WOLF OF BONES

SHIFTER REJECTED SERIES
BOOK FIVE

AMELIA SHAW

CHAPTER I
TALIA

Montana was in the rearview mirror. After Galen received the call about Max's passing, the summit was over for the Long Claw pack. There were no more meetings to attend. No briefings to give, or alliances to be made. Galen had lost the most important ally he'd had—his father. The news hit him hard. It hit us *both* hard.

Max and I had become fast friends in the short time we'd lived together, and I'd taken care of him. Some may have felt the level of care he'd needed was a burden, but I enjoyed our time together. I loved him as if he were my own family and he'd filled the void that had been left in my life after my own father died. The hole in my heart had been ripped wide open once again and even bigger than before.

And the summit wasn't the only thing we'd left behind in our haste to get back home. I left Valerie and Victor in my wake—along with any information they may have had about my mother, her connection to the lost demon princess and my red eyes.

I was *so* close to uncovering the truth about who I was, where I came from and why my eyes turned red without warning. But the timing couldn't have been worse. Galen needed me and I would be there for him no matter what he needed and how long he needed it for. Even if it meant I had to give up on my search for the truth and continued living a lie. I could hold up the charade for as long as I had to if that's what it took to help him through the loss of his father.

Word that Max had succumbed to his mysterious illness spread through the pack bond. Galen's pain reverberated through it, strong enough to call every last Long Claw wolf home to the pack's territory. They soon lined the streets of the main town on either side of the road like a parade route, heads bowed in communal mourning for the loss of one Alpha and to honor another stepping up to lead them in their time of need.

Galen white-knuckled the steering wheel; a muscle in his jaw twitching as he made the turn onto Cypress Lane. The small two-story house Max had called home, with its cut grass and trimmed shrubs, looked the same as it had when Galen backed the truck out of the driveway and first headed for Montana. But despite appearances, nothing would ever be the same again.

I unbuckled my seatbelt, flipped up the center console and slid across the bench seat, leaning against Galen's shoulder.

His muscles relaxed as he rested his head on top of mine and for a brief moment the tension eased from his body. "I don't know if I can do this," he said as he pulled into the drive and parked the truck.

"You can, Galen." I eased back to my side of the truck, pivoting on the bench seat so that I could look at him. "You *can* because you have to." I knew it wasn't what he wanted to hear, but I also knew that he needed to hear it.

Headlights pierced the dark interior of the truck's cab when Theo pulled in behind us. He sat in his car, taking his cue from Galen. He'd step out of the car and head inside when his new Alpha did.

"You don't understand." Galen closed his eyes and exhaled a long breath through his nose. "I'm sorry. I didn't mean... Of course, you understand. It's just—"

"You don't have to explain. I *do* understand. Which means I've been where you are, and I no doubt said the very same things to my friends when my father died. They helped me as much as they could before I left the Northwood pack." I stifled a sob, choking back the emotions that constricted my vocal cords and made it hard to breathe. My chest was tight, and my heart ached, but I forced myself to pull in a deep breath and fill my lungs; composing myself as I let the air out slowly.

"They were there for me. Not as long as I would have liked, but I wouldn't have made it through that first night after my father was killed if it wasn't for them."

Galen pried his fingers from the steering wheel and collapsed across the front seat, resting his head in my lap.

"You can lean on me, Galen." I combed my fingers through his hair, smoothing back the stray locks that fell over his eyes. "I can bear the weight. I'm stronger than you think, and I am here to support you however you need."

"I wish I had half your strength. Talia. After everything you've been through, I don't know how you do it." His tears pooled on my leg and soaked through my jeans. "I don't know how to do this without him."

"Yes, you do." I stroked his hair and slid my hand down to the middle of his back, rubbing small, soothing circles against his coiled muscles. "Your father prepared you for this moment your whole life. He raised you to be the man that you are today, the Alpha of the Long Claw pack. You will lead them through this because it's what your father would have wanted you to do and it's what your pack needs you to do."

"And what about me? Not the heir to the throne and the future Alpha of the Long Claw pack. But me, the man." He pressed his fist against his chest, right over his heart. "When do I get to mourn? When does a son get to say goodbye to his father, if he's already gone?"

"Galen, you need your pack as much as they need you. We're all mourning with you." I turned his head, forcing him to look up at me from my lap. "Take comfort in them. Let them be what gives you the strength to lead. I would have given anything for a pack that mourned my father alongside me."

For the chance to bury him.

"You're right." He scrubbed his hands over his face, sat up and stared out through the windshield at the house where his father had raised him. His hand hovered over the door handle, but he didn't open it.

I hopped out of the truck's cab, walked around the front of the truck and yanked open the driver's side door. "I know you're still doubting your strength right now. I can feel you holding back, trying to keep that uncertainty and self-doubt from seeping into the pack bond." I leaned against the side of the truck and extended my hand. "So, you can borrow some of mine. Come on, we'll do this together."

He dropped out of the truck and grabbed ahold of my hand as tightly as if it were a literal lifeline I'd offered. He laced our fingers together and held on.

The security lights mounted on the corners of the house flipped on as we made our way up the concrete sidewalk that led to the porch where David and Marcus were already waiting to usher us inside. Theo rushed up the walk behind us, taking the front steps two at a time to close the distance and fall in line behind his Alpha.

Apart from the soft glow of the overhead light, mounted above the sink emanating from the kitchen and the warm, yellow glow of the bedside lamp in Max's room spilling out into the hall, the house was dark. But we didn't need light with our enhanced wolf vision. It was as if Max somehow called out to us, his body waiting to be prepared for the funeral service, a magnet that pulled us down the hall and into his room one last time.

Galen dropped into the chair at his father's bedside, rested his elbows on his knees and propped his head in his hands.

His Betas formed a semicircle behind him.

I dutifully moved up and stood at his side.

We stayed with him until the sun peeked through the blinds and the mortician finally came to collect Max's body.

Max's final orders as Alpha for the Long Claw pack had been in relation to the preparation of his funeral service. He gave specific instructions to David and Marcus, handling every last detail so that his son wouldn't have to bear the burden of making the arrangements while working through his grief and assuming the full responsibilities of becoming the new Alpha.

Galen conceded to his father's wishes one last time—even if he didn't agree with the decisions. Still, he adhered to the formal and regimented schedule Max had set for the funeral service. "Lying in state." Galen crumpled the trifold paper program with a full schedule printed within and tossed it in the trash can by the desk in his office at the bar. "This is the part I hate. Is it selfish of me not to want to share this with everyone? There are members of the Long Claw pack that haven't been home in years."

"They just want to pay their respects." I grabbed a bottle of spring water from the mini fridge, along with a protein bar from the bottom of my bag and set them on the desk. "You need to eat," I reminded him.

"They could have paid their respects by being present and accounted for while he was alive," he answered. Galen peeled the wrapper from the granola bar and chucked it in the trash. "And I'm not hungry."

"I know, but you still need to eat. You're no good to anyone if you let yourself get rundown." I nudged the water bottle over the desktop calendar until it brushed his fingertips. "You need to stay hydrated too."

"Thanks." Galen cracked the twist top of the plastic bottle, chugged half the liquid and set it beside the protein bar. He went through the motions. Eating and drinking just enough to keep from being nagged to death by me or his Betas. Galen had run himself ragged fielding calls from allied packs offering their condolences and conference calls with the council. Despite the preparations his father had made, there were still some things Galen just couldn't avoid. And the council was one of them.

Grief and stress had taken their toll on him mentally and physically. He was sleep-deprived and well on his way to being malnourished. The protein bars I stowed in my messenger bag for him weren't nearly enough to maintain a shifter metabolism. He needed to eat a substantial meal and soon.

The refrigerator and freezer at Max's were stocked with meals that pack members had prepared for their new Alpha. Nothing said you cared quite like a casserole. They were all covered in foil, and ready to be popped into the oven, but Galen had no interest in going back to his dads to raid the fridge.

"We should probably head over to the funeral home," I said as I glanced at my phone to check the time. "David, Marcus, and Theo are probably wondering where you are." It had been hours since he'd checked in with his Betas.

Galen had withdrawn bit by bit since he first got the call about Max's death in Montana. I don't think he even realized he was doing it, but it wasn't like him to leave texts and calls unanswered.

"I'm not a hard man to find. If something is wrong, they know where to look." Galen grabbed his suit jacket off the back of the chair and slipped his arms into the sleeves.

"They're worried about you." I held out my hand and pulled him close when he collapsed his hand around mine. "I'm worried about you too." I spared him the lecture of distancing himself from the people who loved him. Given the way I'd handled the problem with my wolf's eyes, I was the last person who needed to be giving a speech about trust and relying on others.

Who wants advice from a hypocrite? Nobody, that's who.

"I know." He brought my hand to his lips and brushed a kiss across my knuckles. "After Jessie died, I spiraled. Marcus, Theo, and David were there for me, but I never would have clawed my way out of the pit I was wallowing in without my dad." Galen pulled his cell out of his back pocket with his free hand and pressed his thumb against the screen to unlock it. It opened to his contacts and Max was at the top of the list.

"When things were good, bad, or in between, he was the person I turned to. I keep reaching for my phone to call him, or for my keys to jump in the truck and drive over there to talk to him."

"My dad and I were close," I offered. "But nothing like you and Max, though he was the one constant in my life. I know what you're going through, and I know it's not the same, but you can always talk to me."

He leaned in and rested his forehead against mine. "It's like there's this hole in the pack bond that nothing will ever fill. I'm hanging on by a thread here. How am I supposed to take care of the pack if I can't even handle going to my own father's funeral?"

"Oh, Galen." I pressed my lips to his in a tender kiss before withdrawing to look into his eyes. "You're handling this the best you can. You're grieving. No one is judging you."

"Maybe not today, but they will." His breath skated across my skin, raising goosebumps when he sighed. "Someone will sense my pain in the bond and take it as a sign of weakness."

"You've been leading them for months now, before your father passed." I cupped his face in my hands. "Look at me, Galen. No one is going to challenge you."

"Someone will. We're shifters, Talia. It's in our nature." He pulled away and stepped out of reach. "We should go."

I wanted to console him, to reassure him that his pack would stand with him and not against him. I wanted to tell him that he was wrong. Except, I'd soon find out he wasn't.

CHAPTER 2
GALEN

We buried our own as was traditional. An Alpha's life was typically violent. Though it all depended on the man and what type of person and leader he was. But an Alpha's death? Violence was all but guaranteed certainty. They fought their way to the top and fought even harder to remain in power once they got there.

It was the norm for an Alpha to die during a pack conflict or a final challenge—not from sickness. It was unheard of. The scars inside an Alpha's body and out, combined with the manner of his death, raised questions. And in my father's case we preferred to keep that out of the public eye. Although, with demons on the loose and rampaging our communities, the secrecy seemed unnecessary.

Old habits die hard.

My father had lived and died as the exception, not the rule. He'd led the Long Claw pack unchallenged until the day he drew his last breath.

First born sons inherited the title and the reins of power when the Alpha died unchallenged or, on in exceedingly rare occasions, retired. In some ways the pack hierarchy functioned like that of a monarchy. While in others it functioned like a cell block in a state prison.

Still, just because a son inherited the title of Alpha, didn't mean they'd get to keep it. Like their fathers before them, anyone with the Alpha title had to fight for it, and more often than not, they lost. Blood relations didn't always imply strength and political dynasties were all but unheard of in our world. Strength was strength and it stood alone. Each potential Alpha had to stand on his own two feet, regardless of his origins or family tree.

The town's only funeral home had three rooms they used for viewings. For my dad's funeral, we reserved them all. The Long Claw pack was smaller than most in the surrounding territories, but my father had been well liked amongst his peers. Friends and allies from neighboring packs came to pay their respects.

The mahogany casket, clear coated and polished to a high shine, sat at the end of the aisle, on top of a metal gurney. White plaster pedestals molded in a Greco-Roman style were situated on either side and topped with two large arrangements of creamy white roses, lilies, and sprigs of pale lavender. A small pulpit stood to the left in invitation for attendees to step up and share their experiences and fond memories.

Talia helped me prepare a speech the night before. The index cards tucked inside my suit jacket felt like lead weights in my pocket. There were so many things I'd wanted to say directly to my dad and would now never have the chance to. Talia had stayed up with me, listening to stories about my dad and the lessons he'd taught me. She'd dutifully collected my thoughts and put pen to paper. And no one would ever hear them, at least no one in this room. Unlike the service, those memories were mine. A piece of my father that belonged to no one else but me, and I would cling to that for as long as possible.

I stepped up to the small podium, but instead of baring my

soul and sharing my grief, I simply thanked everyone for coming and invited them to join us at the pack's cemetery as we buried my father. When the wake ended, the pallbearers—which included David, Marcus, Theo, and myself—carried him from the viewing room and to the hearse which was parked out front, waiting to take my father to his final resting place.

To my relief the majority of the people who'd attended the viewing chose not to attend the graveside service. Their reasons didn't matter to me. I'd done my duty. I'd honored my father's wishes and extended an invitation, willing to welcome anyone who came. And as much as I appreciated their kind words and support at the main service, I didn't want them there in the last moments my father spent above ground. I needed that to be for me.

The pack's private cemetery on our property was in a clearing near the western boundary—a dividing line between our land and the adjacent acres that belonged to our rival, the Northwood pack. Freshly turned earth was piled beside the rectangular hole which had been dug out of the ground. The plot prepared for my father's body.

"Son of a bitch," Talia growled unexpectedly, her hands curled into fists at her side. "Was this what you were talking about this morning?" she growled. "Did you get word that *they* were planning something?"

I followed her steely gaze to a deer trail that cut between a cluster of cedars along the property line.

The Northwood Alpha stepped out of the tree line with his son Maddox in tow. The audacity it took to show their faces at my father's funeral raised my hackles and set me on edge. After everything they'd done to destroy our pack, they had a hell of a lot of nerve to show up right now. And yet, I shouldn't have expected anything less.

Maddox had assaulted Talia and violated the council's

summit treaty. He and his father were more than capable of orchestrating an attack during the service when they no doubt perceived us as being at our most vulnerable as a pack. It was a calculated risk and one that would become a costly mistake for them if they dared.

As a pack we had suffered the loss of our Alpha and our hearts were broken, but our spirits were not. Were we vulnerable? Yes. But did that make us weak? Hell no. My jaw clenched. If Maddox and his father made a move on the Long Claw pack, they would soon find out just how strong we really were.

Nothing unifies a pack quite like a fight.

We would defend my father's honor to the death, but to my surprise the leader and the heir of the Northwood pack never made a move.

Maddox and his father stayed on their side of the property line, heads seemingly bowed in respect for several moments, before they slipped back into the woods and disappeared from sight.

They hadn't come bearing an olive branch of peace and I knew that the cease fire wouldn't last more than one night, but given my father's legacy, I appreciated the gesture, nonetheless. My father had been a great man, and an even greater wolf. He commanded respect, even from his enemies.

I had big shoes to fill, and I just hoped I would be able to live up to the challenge.

Talia and my Betas stayed with me long after the burial service ended and the few pack members that had attended dispersed and headed home.

I stood at my father's graveside, staring down at the top of the coffin that filled the open grave. The creamy white roses tossed in after the service were in stark contrast to the dark lid of the wooden box.

"Galen, it's time." Marcus clasped a hand on my shoulder and jerked his head in the direction of the truck hauling a Bobcat toward the cemetery. "Why don't I give you and Talia a lift back to your place?"

"That would be great, Marcus. Thank you," said Talia as she slipped her hand in mine and pulled me away from the graveside. "This shouldn't be your last memory of him."

I knew she was right. The sight of heavy equipment back-filling dirt on top of the coffin and filling the grave until my father lay six feet under wasn't a memory that I wanted, but I couldn't bring myself to leave. I dug my heels in and remained until the ground was graded and the Bobcat made its last pass.

Talia gently released my hand, pulled a wadded tissue from her purse, dried her red, swollen eyes and dabbed at her nose. Faint streaks of mascara stained her cheeks. She had cried enough tears for both of us while we watched the undertakers finish their work.

I regretted letting her stay but I couldn't afford to let her go. I needed her support now more than ever. The funeral service had to have been particularly painful for her. Not just because she cared for my father, but because she had been denied the opportunity to do the same for her father.

My father's grave was presently unmarked, but a headstone commemorating his life and death would eventually mark the spot of his final resting place. Which was yet another mercy she had been denied by the Northwood pack. Her father lay in an unmarked grave beside her mother.

It was callous and selfish of me to lean on her when her own grief was still so fresh, but she never complained.

She simply steeled her spine and tightened her grip on my hand.

Talia was my rock; the guiding light that I needed to find my way to the other side of my grief. I wouldn't have even made it back to my apartment without her by my side.

My Betas would have propped me up, made sure that I was taking care of myself and helped ease my transition as Alpha. They would have done their best and as much as I would have appreciated it, their best wouldn't have been enough. They shared my pain, but they couldn't understand it—not the way Talia did.

She ushered me from Marcus's car and through the bar.

People dressed in black stood elbow to elbow, glasses and bottles raised in toast to Max, a hell of a guy who was gone too soon and would be missed they said. The crowd's chorus of my father's name followed us up the staircase and out the back of the bar that led to my second-floor apartment.

Talia held the collar of my suit for me, predicting my needs before I expressed them.

I shucked off my jacket and proceeded to drape it over the back of a chair, heaving a heavy sigh.

She grabbed the remote for the sound system and turned up the stereo to drown out the sounds from the bar below.

"Want a drink?" I asked as I moved on autopilot to my personal mini bar. Dropping an oversized ice cube into two bourbon glasses, I poured two fingers of aged oak barrel whiskey into each.

"Come sit with me," Talia called. She had curled up on the couch cushion with one arm draped over the back of the love seat, waiting for me to nestle in beside her.

"To Max," I said and handed her a glass, clinking mine against it. "Salute."

"To Max," Talia echoed, sipping the whiskey before she set her glass on the coffee table. She patted the cushion beside her. "Sit."

I emptied my glass, set it on the table beside her too, and collapsed onto the empty cushion.

"Closer," she coaxed as she grabbed my tie and tugged me over to her side of the loveseat.

I shifted onto my back, legs draped over the arm of the couch and rested my head on her lap.

The tips of her fingers brushed my jaw as she ran her hands through my hair. Her bright violet-blue eyes glistened with unshed tears. We'd been through so much together in such a short amount of time.

I opened the bond I shared with the members of the Long Claw pack as their new Alpha and focused on the connection to the woman beside me. Her pain was so familiar to me. It may as well have been my own and Talia needed to be comforted as much as I did.

Reaching up I cupped the side of her face in one hand and slipped the other around the base of her neck, easing her down until her lips brushed mine. She smelled of vanilla with a hint of whiskey on her breath and I wanted nothing more than to lose myself in her scent and essence at that moment.

Talia kissed me, mewling with pleasure when I not only returned the kiss but deepened it. She loosened my tie and slipped it off my neck, before moving to the buttons on my crisp, white button-down dress shirt.

I pulled back from the kiss and sat up, shedding my clothes before helping remove hers, until we were skin-to-skin without a shred of fabric left between us. She was soft, warm, and everything I needed.

We took our time, savoring each other; exploring each other's bodies as if for the first time all over again. Any other time, the slow tease would have driven me crazy with need, but this was more than raw passion. It wasn't just the heat of the moment or pure desire. It was something more. It was love and caring.

When I fell in love with Talia, I'd fallen hard. I thought I'd been in love before, but even the feelings I'd had for Jessie truly paled in comparison to what I felt for Talia. It was unlike anything I'd ever experienced before.

I felt a fleeting pang of guilt and grief for the loss of a woman that I'd once cared for. We were young, foolish, and carefree at the time. I'd thought she was my mate and I'd mourned her as if she were—swearing off any other mating when she died. But then I met Talia.

She broke through the barrier I'd built around my heart without even trying. Talia completed me and through the pack bond I knew she felt the same way. She owned me body and soul. With a strength that was uniquely her own, she reached down through the darkness that threatened to take hold of my heart and pulled me back into the light. Talia thought I'd saved her, but in truth it was the other way around.

And it didn't matter that she had been destined for another. Fate was wrong, I knew it unequivocally. I needed her more than I needed air. Talia was meant for me, and I would do whatever it took to make her mine for the rest of our lives.

CHAPTER 3
TALIA

"I never would have thought this was possible." I traced lazy circles across Galen's bare chest with my index finger. "I was a fated mate, or at least that's what I was told... but the bond I shared with Maddox was nothing like this. I mean, looking back there wasn't really a bond at all. Of course, we never—" I swallowed the rest of the sentence.

"I thought Jessie was my fated mate," Galen said to fill in the silence. "She never bore the mark, but we both woke up every day assuming it would appear on her arm at some point." Galen took my hand in his and brought it to his lips, brushing a kiss across the tips of my fingers. "But it never did."

"A mark?" I murmured, almost under my breath, though Galen would have heard it as clearly as if I'd spoken with more volume.

"You never received the mark when you and Maddox were together?" Galen asked as he snaked his arm over my hip and around my back, drawing me close as if he feared I'd try to run away from him and the conversation.

Not that I haven't given him reason to feel that way to be fair.

I had been keeping secrets. I'd been rejected once and had no desire to experience that pain all over again. There were things that I wasn't ready to share—like the color of my wolf's eyes or the visit from the Alaskan wolves—Valerie and Victor—before we left the summit.

But as for my relationship, or lack thereof, with Maddox? There wasn't anything Galen could have asked that I wouldn't be able and willing to provide an honest answer for. "No." I flattened my palm against his chest, over his heart, and took comfort in its steady rhythm. "I just believe it to be true. Everyone said we were. My father, his father, the pack accepted it as truth. In fact, I can't remember a time when I wasn't referred to as Maddox's fated mate. It was like part of the pack canon, and I never gave the lack of a mark a second thought."

"It's unusual, given the Northwood Alpha's disdain for you, that he would be so certain you would be fated to marry his son." Galen rested his forehead against mine, the warmth of his breath sending shivers down my spine.

"It is, isn't it?" I'd never really thought of it that way before... However, if I had any doubt at all about Maddox's feelings for me, he'd made them crystal clear at the summit. He'd never loved me. He loathed me. Anger, disgust, hate was what he truly felt, and all of those emotions boiled just beneath the surface. It was no wonder, with the way his father felt about me.

Still, Maddox had given an award-winning performance before that, in the lead up to our end. For years he'd led me to believe he was head-over-heels in love with me. That I was his one and only fated mate. But it wasn't true. It couldn't have been. All the signs were there, or the lack thereof. My life with the Northwood pack had been nothing but a lie.

I'd thought I was in love with Maddox, but I was far too young and naive to know any better. With nothing to compare it to, it was all too easy for my ex-fiancé to convince me that he was my destiny. Ignorance had been bliss, back then. At least for a little while.

But I wouldn't trade the pain of being expelled from my pack, of being cut out of Maddox's life or of learning the truth, for anything. Every tear I'd shed had led me to Galen and helped give life to the love we felt for each other now.

I wasn't sure why Maddox or his father had been so hell-bent on marrying me into their family. I could only suppose it was another way to control me and my father. And when that didn't work, they'd murdered him and cast me out in the blink of an eye.

Without stopping to think I'd spent so much time and energy hating them, when in reality I should have been grateful all along. Not marrying Maddox was the best thing that could have ever happened to me.

Next to meeting Galen.

"I know this is going to sound crazy, Talia, but I know in my heart that you *are* my fated mate. You have to be." Galen tightened his hold on me, our bodies molded together.

"I feel it too, Galen, but..." The words wedged themselves between a sob and the back of my throat like a choking wedge. "There's no mark."

"I don't give a shit about a mark," he said adamantly. "I know what I feel. It's right there in the bond. You're my mate, Talia." Galen sounded so sure of himself and the connection between us.

But that's because he doesn't know the truth—the whole truth.

Everything he felt was based on the person he thought I was. Not the red-eyed freak I'd become. Would he have fallen in love with a demon-eyed wolf? As much as I wanted to believe the answer was 'yes', I feared the answer would in fact be a resounding no.

I'm a hypocrite!

I'd spent months condemning Maddox and his father for the lies they'd ensnared me with. Yet here I was curled up on the couch with Galen entangling him in my own web of lies. The difference though in my situation, was that it wasn't meant with malice or the goal to manipulate him. I wanted to tell Galen the truth so badly, but I was afraid right to my very soul. I didn't have enough information just yet. I'd reveal it *all* once I understood who and what I truly was, but until then...

"I want to believe that" I said. "I want to *be* that, more than anything." I buried my head in the crook of his neck, hiding the unshed tears glistening in my eyes from his view.

"After everything the Northwood pack put you through, I can understand why you'd have your doubts." He nuzzled into my hair and breathed in my scent. "It's okay, Talia. I believe it enough for the both of us." He adjusted his position on the couch, shifting me beneath him in one fluid move and wedged himself firmly between my legs. "In the meantime, I'll do whatever it takes to prove that we're fated mates to you and everyone else." Galen's voice dropped to a husky, primal baritone that raised goosebumps across my skin.

"Whatever it takes?" I rasped, my heart racing and anticipation coiling within me.

"What can I say, I'm a dedicated man in love." He trailed kisses down my neck and slid his hands beneath the hem of my black dress, inched it up my thighs and proved what a dedicated man he truly was. He hooked his thumbs beneath the thin straps of my bikini-cut silk panties, slid them down my legs and over my feet, then tossed them over his shoulder onto the floor. His fingers left a wake of fire on my sensitive skin as they kneaded their way up my calf.

Every cell in my body was electrified by his touch. Anticipation built into a heady mix of pleasure and pain. I needed Galen as much as I needed air to breathe.

Maybe more.

He pressed his hand against my knee, spreading my legs

further apart and buried his face between my thighs. He devoured me, lavishing and suckling at my core so intensely that it brought me to the very edge of climax.

Somehow, by sheer force of will I managed to hold back. I desperately needed to feel him inside me. I'd been craving the way the hard length of him filled me up when I tumbled over the edge and into ecstasy.

But he gripped my hips, digging his fingers into my flesh, and held me in place when I attempted to move out from under him to switch positions. Galen was relentless in his pursuit of my orgasm, only stopping when his name tore from my lips in a hoarse scream.

I lay there, trembling, and unable to move; my muscles weak from another first with the man who had just claimed me body and soul.

"You're my mate, Talia." A primal growl built in the back of Galen's throat, heightening my arousal even though I had just orgasmed. "Look at me," he demanded.

I held his gaze as he eased inside me, muscles contracting around every inch of him until his hips pressed against mine. My eyes flitted closed once more and I gasped at the pleasure edged by delicious pain as he buried himself inside me.

"Open your eyes, Talia. I want you to look at me while I claim you." His words were enough to send me tumbling back over the cliff and into oblivion. "Tell me you love me. I want to hear you say it."

I fell for Galen, and I fell hard. "I love you," I breathed, meaning the words with every ounce of my being.

He rocked his hips, the slow rhythm increasing with each stroke until he was driven by raw need and reached a fevered and frantic pace. It was wilder and rougher than our first time together and I was certain I would be sore tomorrow, but I didn't care. It felt amazing.

Any lingering aches and pains I might experience in the morning would be worth it. Losing myself with him in this moment was exactly what I needed—what Galen needed—and I took pleasure in knowing that we could give that to each other.

"Are you okay?" Regret flickered in his eyes before he collapsed on top of my chest and buried his face in the crook of my neck. "I lost control. I shouldn't have..." he began.

I pressed my index finger to his lips as he rose, silencing the rest of his unnecessary apology. "I'm better than okay, Galen."

How could I not be? He just claimed me.

Granted it was in the throes of passion as opposed to a declaration made in front of the entire pack, but there was no denying the connection between us. I felt a change in the energy of the pack bond. Besides, a formal announcement before all of the pack members didn't necessarily mean anything. That had been a lesson I'd learned the hard way—when Maddox broke off our engagement.

"Do you feel that?" Galen rolled off me onto his side, took my hand in his and placed it over his heart. "My heart beats like that whenever I'm around you."

"I think your rapid heartbeat has more to do with what we were just doing than it does me," I teased, tracing his well-defined pecs with my fingertips.

"You have no idea the hold you have over me." He wrapped his arm around my waist and pulled me tight against him, our bodies melding together. "I just wish my father had lived long enough for me to tell him that I found my mate."

"He knew, Galen," I whispered as I rested my face on the pillow beside his and brushed my lips against his in a gentle kiss. "I'm pretty sure he knew how we felt about each other long before either of us truly did."

"Yeah." A somber laugh escaped him. "I suppose he did. He

called me out on my feelings for you right from the beginning, but I was too stubborn to hear it. If I'd just listened to him sooner..."

"Don't do that. Between the Northwood pack, the demon's curse on the witches, and their attacks on the town, it's a wonder we've made it this far." I draped my leg over his hip and hooked my heel around the back of his thigh, entwining our bodies together. "I mean, our timing couldn't have been worse."

"I don't know. I think we met exactly when we were supposed to. If our paths crossed even a week earlier, the outcome would have been very different." Galen licked and nipped my neck and the warmth of his breath sent shivers down my spine.

"You would have hated me. You'd likely have begged me to take you back to Maddox and the Northwood pack."

"It must be fate then," I said. Tilting my head to the side, I granted him better access to the sensitive skin along my collarbone.

"There's not a doubt in my mind," he answered. Galen's hands roamed my body, fanning the flames of my desire yet again. The evidence of his arousal grew while we cuddled and pressed against my stomach, threatening me with a good time. He rolled onto his back, then, and pulled me on top of him, guiding my hips as he sheathed himself inside me for the second time.

"You are my fate, Talia." Galen rocked his hips and drove himself into me from below, deeper and more aggressively, until we were both up and over the precipice of ecstasy and climaxing together, vocalizing our love in the way only two wolf shifters can.

I prayed to any gods that may have been listening that Galen was right and we were fated, because there was only one mark on my arm. And that mark belonged to a demon.

CHAPTER 4
TALIA

The Alpha who had given me life and guided me was dead, but the world somehow kept turning. It seemed cruel that life marched on without my father, but I found solace in the imprint he left behind on our pack. There were glimpses of him everywhere around me—if I knew where to look for them.

And Talia always made sure that I did. She used the expansion of the bond between us to feel out my mood and searched for examples of my father's guiding hand among my wolves whenever I needed it most. She soothed me in a way that felt effortless, and we fell into an easy rhythm. With each day that passed my belief that Talia and I were meant to be together was solidified.

Her presence in my life was fate—it had to be—whether she believed it or not. I certainly had my work cut out in convincing her, though. A fated mark had yet to appear on her arm, and she took that as a bad omen, especially after being convinced while growing up that Maddox was her fated mate.

I honestly wished I'd never mentioned a fated mark to her at all, but the fact that she'd never had one with Maddox felt like

24

more proof in my mind that she was meant for me. If only she believed the same. But we loved each other and that was enough —for the time being.

Truth be told, we had our hands full to overflowing with increased demon activity and a new wave of attacks to dwell too much on the intricacies of our relationship. Things had ramped up after my father's funeral. It was almost as if his death and the attacks were connected, but no matter how I tried to figure it out, for the life of me I couldn't understand how. My father hadn't conjured, nor ever been marked by a demon.

Still, there was no denying a correlation to his illness, the demon attacks, Talia's arrival, and her demon mark. It felt like an array of various puzzle pieces were spread out before me, but regardless of how I arranged them, I couldn't make them all fit.

One evening I was seated at my bar, pondering my dad's illness and how it might fit with the rest of what was going on with the attacks, when my phone danced across the counter with an incoming call from Theo.

"There's been another attack," he managed, before he broke off to shout orders to another wolf in the background. It was something about securing the property line. I couldn't place whose voice it was over our shoddy cell connection.

"Think of the devil and a demon will appear," I muttered, sliding off my stool and heading around behind the bar to grab my keys.

"What?" Theo asked, sounding confused by my remark.

"Nothing. I'm on my way." I'd spent more time working and sleeping at the bar since we buried my father, but it was only a short drive back to the pack's land. I contemplated grabbing Talia from the bedroom upstairs to accompany me, but she'd been so tired since we buried my dad that in the end, I decided not to disturb her. The death of my father and Alpha—her friend —had dredged up a lot of memories about losing her own father,

I knew. She needed a moment's peace and rest. I could handle this.

Eight minutes and three tripped red-light cameras later, I pulled up to the gate that separated the Northwood property from the rest of town.

A shifter stepped out from under the cover of the evergreens that lined the property, unlocked the heavy chain and swung open the metal gate.

Darius.

"Theo and Marcus are already waiting for you at the northeastern marker," Darius said as he raised two fingers to his brow in a mock salute, then moved to secure the gate as soon as I drove through.

A plume of dust kicked up behind the truck as I veered down the dirt road at double the posted speed limit for the main drag that wound its way through our small community. My trio of Betas came into view as I rounded the bend toward the property marker. "Shit." The cab jerked forward and back when I slammed on the brakes and threw the truck into park. I hopped out of the truck, headlights glaring and engine still running, and ran at a full clip to join my Betas at the scene of the attack.

Fallen trees and broken branches littered the ground. It looked like a tornado had ripped through the woods that had always created a natural barrier between our property and the Northwood pack's land. The ground was mounded in some places, splintered and cracked in others, as if the demons had burst through the soil itself in a surprise attack.

The witches who had set up home on our pack's lands had crafted a magical ward around our property to keep the demons out. They routinely reinforced it on a weekly basis, rotating through members of the coven to ensure their magic wasn't depleted and the ward remained intact. They worked hard to keep us all safe while honoring our alliance.

But the demons had obviously worked harder—at least in this instance. They were relentless in their attempts to destroy the magic shield around our property and occasionally those attempts proved successful. This was one of those times.

"Casualties?" I rushed to join my Betas, leaping over a narrow chasm that had been ripped open in the earth.

The smell of blood and brimstone hit me the second my feet hit the other side of the crevice. My eyes, nose, and the back of my throat burned from the combination of copper and sulfur that coated the inside of my mouth and clung to my sinuses.

"Pam took at least half a dozen with broken bones and lacerations up to the meeting hall to recover." He wiped blood and dirt from his eyes with the hem of his charcoal gray t-shirt. "The rest..."

I followed his gaze to a pile of bodies strewn beneath the trees. "Damn it." I growled, my partially shifted claws piercing my palms as my hands curled into fists at my sides. "The witches plug one hole in the ward and the demons simply create another. How the hell are we going to stop them?" The question was rhetorical, but Marcus answered anyway.

"We need to find *their* weakness and take the battle to them before they wipe us out, Galen." Marcus squatted down at the edge of the massive crack in the ground and stared into the black depths as if he could see the demons down below.

"Don't you think I'm working on that?" My lip curled, baring elongated canines.

My wolf paced just beneath the surface, ready to force the shift and burst through my skin in a terrifying display of fur and fang. But there was no one left to fight. Our enemies had done what they'd come to do and fled the scene equally as fast. It's like their sole purpose was destruction for destruction's sake. It made no fucking sense.

I held onto my rage by a mere thread. I feared that if I lost my control now, I would never get it back.

"Easy, Boss." David moved to stand between Marcus and me as if sensing my wrath.

With no enemies to fight, my wolf sought out the next best thing and Marcus was the strongest of my Betas. My wolf sensed the inherent strength in him that made him the perfect choice to act as my second in command and directed all of our anger and frustration at him in the form of a challenge.

Marcus was wise enough not to accept. "Alpha." Marcus took a submissive stance, bowed his head and spoke softly and slowly. "We need to bury the bodies."

"Some of the pack members are afraid the dead will attract more demons," added David as he mirrored Marcus's posture.

I turned my still-irate gaze on him. "That's ridiculous." I sounded more animal than man as I battled my wolf for control of my body. "If that were true, the town's morgue would be ground zero for demon activity. The families need to be notified and given time to arrange proper burials," I growled.

"Galen, we don't have time..." Theo broke off and dropped to one knee when I fixed my partially shifted eyes on him.

"We are not fucking savages!" I roared as I slammed my eyes closed, chest heaving. I sucked in breath after deep breath of air and forced my wolf to back down with everything I had. Finally, I opened my eyes to gaze upon my men. "Notify the families."

All three Beta's moved, but at a snail's pace. They knew to tread lightly when I was in this condition.

I knew what needed to be done to keep the peace among the pack, but that didn't mean I liked it. The problem with near immortality was that the age gap between our wolves was wider than the Grand Canyon. As a result, some wolves clung to the old ways and superstitions. And with demons roaming the earth it was hard to blame them. These were unprecedented times.

"We'll prepare a funeral pyre," I called after them, offering the idea as a concession. "That will be a more effective use of our time. Just let their families know that a proper memorial will be erected in their honor once we've eradicated the demon scourge." I gave my final instructions and left it up to my Betas to decide amongst themselves which of them would carry out my wishes while I put in a call to Marguerite.

The coven leader readily agreed to bring members of her coven to repair the breach in the ward and help us with a funeral pyre that would be worthy of the wolves who'd sacrificed their lives to protect the rest of our pack.

Obviously decided on their course of action, Marcus and David sprinted across the field, breaking into a full run when they reached the road that led back to the meeting hall. Theo stayed behind, most likely to keep an eye on me and make sure I didn't wolf out while I waited for the witches to arrive.

Within minutes, Marguerite, Sarah, and several other witches appeared and set to work repairing the ward. Once the tear in the magic had been patched, they knelt before my fallen wolves and offered up a prayer to their goddess for the protection of their souls beyond the Veil.

"I am sorry, Galen." Marguerite bowed at the waist and offered her condolences. "You and your wolves have given so much to protect us all from the demons, but somehow, they're getting stronger. There's only so much my girls and I can do. Our magic is not without limits."

"No one blames you, Marguerite," I said, wanting to reassure the high priestess, but fell short with my clipped words and harsh tone.

"Alpha," Marguerite said as she lowered the hood on her cloak and met my gaze. "If you wish for me and my coven to leave your lands, there will be no ill will between us. We have each repaid our debts to one another in kind."

"I'm not rescinding my invitation any time soon, Marguerite. You and the coven are welcome here." I raked my fingers through my hair and sighed. "I had just hoped my father's funeral would be the last one for the pack. At least for a little while, you know?"

"All too well, my friend." She clasped a hand on my shoulder and briefly shared in the burden of my grief, one leader to another. "All too well," she repeated.

Faced with the death of several more pack members it was easy to forget that Marguerite had suffered more losses among her coven than our pack had. Their initial losses had been devastating—it was why I agreed to take them in and forge the alliance in the first place.

Marcus and David returned with the victims' families in a caravan of vehicles. The four of us stood by their sides, remaining steadfast as the magical-fueled funeral pyre burned bright. Words were shared and tears were shed while Marguerite and the coven tended to the bodies, before they were transferred to the flames for a burning the likes of which ancient Vikings would have been proud.

I waited until the last magical ember had lost its reddish glow and turned an ashen black before leaving the dead to their peace and drove back across town; back to my apartment above the bar where Talia likely anxiously awaited my return.

What awaited me when I stepped into my living space wasn't the greeting I'd expected.

She'd been on an emotional rollercoaster since joining my pack and had hardly had a moment to herself to grieve the loss of her own father—let alone mine. And so there she sat on the floor sobbing, curled up in a ball with her thighs tucked against her chest and arms locked around her shins. Rather than raise her gaze to greet me, she buried her head behind her knees when I opened the door.

"Talia, hey. Look at me." I kneeled on the floor in front of her and tried to coax her out of her defensive pose. "Tell me what's wrong, baby. Talk to me. I'm here."

I felt confident I knew what was bothering her. Burying my father had torn open a freshly healed wound and had been a painful reminder of what she'd been deprived of by the Northwood pack after their Alpha murdered her dad. Still, I wanted her to open up to me. I needed her to know she could truly trust me.

Talia had been my shoulder to cry on when I'd required it. She'd listened whenever I needed someone to talk to. And I wanted more than anything to be that for her in return, but she was refusing to let me in. Something had been eating away at her like a slow poison since before we left for the summit, and I wanted to know what the hell it was.

How can I help her if she refuses to speak? We have enough problems on our hands as a pack without my mate keeping secrets.

I sighed heavily. "Talia, I've tried to be caring, I've tried to be kind, but enough is enough. I'm tired of dancing around your secrets. You are going to tell me what is going on with you. Tonight." I raked my fingers through my hair, shaking ash from the funeral pyre loose from the tangled strands in frustration.

She poked her head up and gazed at me with puffy red eyes; tears streaming down her cheeks, but never spoke a single word.

"I thought we'd made progress," I said. "I thought that we were past this." I pressed my palms against my eyes and willed my wolf to stay in the shadows of my mind. We were both raw and on edge after facing the devastation and death the demons had left in their wake. Talia shutting us out *again* was more than my wolf and I could bear. It physically hurt and I'd had enough pain for one day.

"Fine. You don't want to tell me?" I opened myself up to the Alpha bond I shared with the pack and tugged on the thread that connected me to Talia, putting pressure on it, willing her to reveal her truth. "I have other ways of getting the information I need if that is your choice."

She gasped and tried to close herself off from the bond, reinforcing the mental walls she'd built inside her mind to safeguard her secrets.

I'd never played the Alpha card or used the bond that way—because I'd never had to. But her refusal to share all of herself with me—the bad as well as the good—struck a heavy blow to not only my heart and pride, but *also* my trust.

Despite my conviction, remorse soon set in the moment I saw the look of horror in her eyes and my own gaze reflected back at me in the depths of hers. It was all too much, too soon. Admitting my feelings for Talia, burying my father and several pack members all in the same week? I was in turmoil. I was a proverbial bundled mess of emotions.

But that was no excuse to invade her privacy like this. No matter how I sliced it, I'd crossed a line—a line that I'd drawn and sworn never to cross. Talia wrecked me, but there was no one to blame for my actions but myself. I'd let my anger get the better of me and I'd no doubt fractur whatever trust she's had in me. "Fuck!" I growled as I dug my keys out of my pocket and stormed out of the apartment, slamming the door behind me.

My boots pounded against the steps as I stomped my way down to the bar. I needed some air and a stiff drink. I stalked across the room, grabbed a bottle of tequila from the top shelf and stowed away to my office in the back. I threw open the window, sucking in deep breaths of the cool night air while guzzling down the high-priced liquid gold. Half a bottle of the caramel-colored liquor later, my temper had subsided, and a throbbing headache had taken its place.

But the physical pain was a welcome reprieve from its emotional counterpart and helped cut through the red haze of anger which had been clouding my vision since I'd been forced to resort to burning the bodies of our dead. The last time I'd felt that out of control and helpless was when Jessie had died.

And that was the connection right there. More senseless deaths that I couldn't prevent and situations that were outside my control; made worse by the fact that I was the Alpha and clearly failing at my primary job of keeping the pack safe and happy.

As much as I wanted to know what was going on with Talia, she didn't deserve a show of force like the power flex I'd made her to endure up there in my apartment. I needed to earn her trust, I needed to be patient and wait until she was ready to spill out her heart... it wasn't something I could demand. And that was my mistake. One that I couldn't take back. On top of that, I'd gone and made it worse by walking out on her to drown my own sorrows. I wasn't there for her at all.

Another promise broken.

·CHAPTER 5
TALIA

I *screwed up! Fuck.*

Galen had come home and caught me in a moment of weakness. And rather than open up to the man I loved, I closed myself off in fear. I knew Galen wasn't prying or trying to hurt me. In fact, it was the exact opposite. I knew it in my bones that he wanted nothing more than to help me; to take care of me. Which is what normal people did when they were in a healthy relationship—something with which I'd had little experience.

My father had *never* opened up to me about any of the important things. He hadn't told me about his and my mother's past, and my engagement to Maddox had been a lie right from the start to its finish. So, it's what I was used to... lies and deception were something I had plenty of experience with, for better or worse. That element of my own past I had no control over.

But I'd been lying to Galen for weeks, now. He'd given me the space I'd asked for, and then some, while in return all I did was build lie upon lie until I'd forced his hand to use the bond to pry his way into my thoughts. I was the one at fault and it burned me to my core. If only I could bring myself to confide in him, to tell him the truth about my red eyes, and my strange origins...

I can't lose him. What am I going to do? He's already dealing with so much! I don't want to add to his burden, but it seems I already have.

When he'd threatened to use the bond before we left for the summit, I knew that he was bluffing. This time, I knew he wasn't.

Galen wanted the truth, that was all. And he deserved the truth, but it would take a lot for him to violate my trust or jeopardize our relationship in that way.

Something must have happened when he was called away on pack business this time.

He'd dealt with any number of demon attacks before, but I'd never seen him react this way. Whatever it was, I'd felt it ruminating through our connection while he was gone and then picked up on his distress when he'd walked through the door.

But he'd taken one look at me and the state I was in and put his feelings aside—and then I'd made a selfish fool of myself with my stubborn silence. So, in desperation and emotional turmoil he'd tapped the bond, shocking me, but I held him back just long enough for him to see through the hurt and anger I'd caused by keeping myself closed off from him.

And then he stormed out. He was only one floor away—I could sense that he was still inside the building, which likely meant he was downstairs in his office—but there might as well have been a thousand miles separating us. I had no idea how to fix what I'd just broken and the guilt was eating me alive, adding to the taint of the demon's claim on me. It seemed like everything I touched, I destroyed one way or another...

They say time heals all wounds... and I hoped and prayed that would be true for us, too; because I couldn't imagine my life without Galen in it. I didn't want to. The mere thought was unbearable after everything we'd been through together.

My wolf paced within me, begging to be let free. She was

anxious and needed to run, but I couldn't let her out and risk Galen finding out the truth on his own without an explanation. *I needed to be the one to tell him.* If only I'd had the courage to do it before I broke his trust and forced his hand.

The clunk of Galen's boots hitting the treads echoed in the stairway on the other side of the door. I watched the knob turn for what felt like an eternity before he walked through the doorway with his shoulders hunched and head hung low.

"I called a pack meeting," he said. "I'm heading back there now. You're welcome to join me if you want." He stared at the floor, refusing to look at me. "But if you prefer to take your car and go on your own, I'll understand. After the way I treated you, I wouldn't blame—"

"Of course, I'll go with you." I grasped at the olive branch he'd extended and jumped up from the same spot on the floor I'd been sitting on when he stomped out. "Let me just grab my purse."

Galen waited on the landing, holding the door open for me; his body tensing when I brushed past and bounded down the stairs.

We rode to the Northwood property in suffocating silence, the tension building between us with each street we passed until I couldn't bear it any longer and managed to make an awkward apology of sorts.

"I don't know why I'm like this, Galen. But please know it has *nothing* to do with you." I emptied my lungs, exhaling the breath I'd been holding since we turned onto the private road that led to the pack's property. "I'll tell you everything when I can, when I'm ready. I promise. Just please don't let this come between us."

"I don't want this to come between us either, Talia." Galen spared a glance in my direction before returning his attention back to the road. "But I also don't want there to be any secrets between us."

That's more than reasonable.

"I know." I sighed and pressed my fingers against my eyes to stem the flow of tears that threatened to fall. "It's just— I think I'm ready to share this with you and then my anxiety gets the better of me ..." I trailed off, shrugging. "I'm scared."

Galen sighed. "I love you, Talia, and I want you to share everything with me. The good, the bad, the ugly. It doesn't matter. Your problems are *my* problems. You need to know that." He gripped the steering wheel, knuckles white under the strain. "I know I did a piss poor job of proving that earlier. Tonight has been... well, it's been shit and I let my temper get the better of me. I'm sorry for what I almost did. I shouldn't have invaded your privacy like that."

"I'm sorry too." I offered immediately, reaching across the cab of the truck to rest my hand on his thigh. "I'll try and find my courage. But until then, can we just start tonight over?"

"If it's all the same to you, I'd rather just forget this night ever happened." Galen's lips mashed together in a straight line and his jaw muscle twitched, before he let me in on what had happened earlier. It was yet another breach of the pack land's perimeter by demons. And he'd barely held it together in relation to his temper, apparently.

His sour mood had nothing to do with me. So, that time I knew not to take it personally. Just like he seemed to know not to press me anymore regarding discussing my secret. We'd learned a hard lesson together, but at the same time we both knew things couldn't continue the way they were.

If I wanted a life with Galen—and I did, desperately—I had to come clean. The sooner the better. But all the things I wanted to say had to wait until after the pack meeting... but I would say them, regardless of the consequences.

Galen had enough on his mind and on his plate. He didn't need the added stress of my troubles right before he was set to speak to the entire pack. He needed to focus on the needs of the many, not the needs of one. After the meeting, when he'd concluded his obligations to the pack for the night, we'd have time *alone* to talk. I could finally try and fix things before they got any worse.

I still wasn't quite sure why he'd needed to call the meeting in the first place. It was obvious he'd come back to the apartment in need of comfort after the funeral pyre. He'd needed a safe place to share his feelings and experiences, a person to bounce ideas off of.

He needed his mate.

And I needed to do better. I couldn't let fear rule me anymore or it would destroy us. Maddox hadn't shared his true thoughts of feelings with me. And I'd certainly never been privy to his or his father's plans, and my opinion had never counted for anything. I was merely the arm candy, the beautiful wolf selected to stand by his side. No more, no less.

On the other hand, Galen saw me as a true partner. He not only listened to what I had to say, but he valued my opinion. Even when he didn't always agree with it. He treated me the way I imagined was the right way to be treated. But it felt so foreign to me. My experience with love and relationships had been limited to Maddox, so I had zero experience when it came to demonstrating real commitment with Galen. Everything was so new, so different, and I was learning on the go.

We'd just had our first real fight, and we'd managed to come back together, each apologizing without demanding it of the other. I could only hope for the same outcome when he learned what I had to say after the meeting.

Galen honked the horn in a pattern of short and long bursts which reminded me of morse code. The main gate swung open as the headlights rounded the last bend before the entrance to the property. "I'm glad you decided to ride with me," he said as he veered the truck to the right and toward the meeting hall.

"Me too, even if I haven't been very good company." I tugged at the seatbelt that rode up my shoulder and across my neck and shifted in my seat to face him. In fact, other than apologizing for my part in our argument, I hadn't said much of anything the whole drive. I'd been lost in my own thoughts about all the things I planned to say to him later that night.

I promised him that I'd find my courage—and I will.

"Just having you with me is enough."

My heart melted in an instant and I smiled for the first time all night.

Galen drove the truck around to the back of the meeting hall and parked the truck next to Theo's car. "I really need you by my side in there," he admitted, squeezing my hand.

"There's no place I'd rather be," I told him truthfully before opening the passenger side door. I hopped out of the cab, earth crunching beneath my feet, and came around the front of the truck to join him.

We entered the meeting hall side by side, hand in hand, like a celebrity power couple, but I was all too aware of Galen's trepidation through our bond. Whatever he planned to say, it was obviously a major announcement. Steeling my nerves, I followed him through the community kitchen and out into the main meeting room.

A hush fell over the crowd and the pack dipped their heads in a show of respect for their new Alpha as Galen moved through the room and took his place behind a small lectern positioned in the front of the large hall. "Thank you all for coming out tonight on such short notice." Galen's voice boomed throughout the open space. "I'm sure by now most of you have heard about the losses we suffered during the demon attack tonight."

A pang of fresh guilt washed over me. I'd been at Galen's crying over my own problems, worrying about myself while the pack was under attack and wolves had died. I felt ashamed, but kept a stoic expression, revealing nothing of my problems to the rest of the pack. Instead, I put my regrets aside and listened to our Alpha as he explained in more detail exactly what had happened.

"First, I need to thank everyone who stepped up tonight to tend our wounded and assist the witches with the remains of our fallen." Galen skipped over the gorier details of the attack to spare the younger wolves who had attended the meeting with their parents but got his story across soberly all the same.

"I've spoken with Marguerite and moving forward, there will be a witch on patrol every shift. I know we've had a few attacks here on the property, but with the wards the witches have created, it's still safer here than in town. I'm asking those of you who live off pack lands to consider moving back home—at least for the time being."

Galen raised his hands, gesturing to the crowd to simmer down as he aimed to quell the rising tide of concerned voices. "We are safer and stronger together as a pack. I am more than proud of each and every one of you for the contributions you have made as members of the Long Claw pack. And it's in that spirit that I stand here before you today to ask for your support, to stay the course and fight with me against the demons until we can end this."

My old Alpha never would have addressed the Northwood pack that way. He wouldn't have asked for help; he would have simply demanded it. He believed in might over right, in aggression over compassion. But that's how Galen was different and how he maintained the respect of his wolves—by giving them the respect and support they deserved. He always offered them a choice.

"I know you're all tired. I share your pain and grief. I feel it through the pack bonds and in my heart as if it were my own." He paused before forging ahead. "Remember what my father always said: 'There is strength in numbers, but the real power is in unity.' We've all lost parents, brothers, sisters, and loved ones, but I won't let their deaths be in vain. You have my solemn vow."

Galen ended the meeting with new perimeter patrol rotations, the promise of safety protocols for the pack and coven to follow shortly, along with the renewed support of his pack.

When the meeting adjourned and the pack began to disperse out the doors, Galen turned to me. "I want to run the property line and check in with Marguerite before we head back to the bar. Do you want to come with me, or..." He let the unspoken question hang between us, no doubt expecting my answer would be 'no'.

I hadn't joined him on a run since the Northwood pack's last attempt at a takeover—and the first appearance of my red eyes.

It's now or never, Talia.

The invitation to go for a run provided the perfect segue to come clean with Galen. "Yes, I'd love to join you," I said, offering him a small smile.

A flicker of hope flashed in Galen's eyes, and I almost regretted my decision. As much as I hated the idea of being rejected *again*—or worse, hurting Galen—it was too late to back out. For better or worse I'd just agreed to go on a run and had no rational reason for changing my mind. There would be no backing out now.

"But if it's okay with you, I need to tell you something first. You might decide to rescind that invitation after you hear what I have to say." My heart raced and my stomach roiled. Swallowing the lump in my throat, I took his silence as an invitation to continue. "You asked what's bothering me on multiple occasions and I've given you the same answer every time. *Nothing.* But all along you've known it was something."

I took a deep breath and plowed ahead, terrified I'd lose my nerve if I allowed him to interrupt. It appeared he felt the same way because he didn't move a muscle or utter a single word. I was pretty sure he was holding his breath at this point, too.

"I can't imagine what's going through your mind right now. What do you think I might be about to say. I just hope whatever it is, it's worse than what I have to tell you and that everything I say will feel like a relief. If you're worried it's about us, don't be. I'm still very much in love with you, Galen. As much, if not more so than when you claimed me."

Cracks in Galen's statuesque demeanor appeared, and his coiled muscles relaxed slightly. It was clear from his posture that he was worried my issues and secrets were about us.

I cleared my throat and began. "After the Northwood pack attacked us and I stood up to my old Alpha, you found me down by the water; do you remember?"

The question was rhetorical, but he nodded in affirmation.

"Something happened when I shifted that night." I swallowed hard before blurting out what I'd been hiding for months—the proverbial thorn in my paw. "My eyes turned red, Galen. And it's happened since, but it only seems to happen when I'm in my wolf form. I've replayed the events from that night over and over in my head and nothing stands out as a cause or explanation. And I've been so afraid. I just don't know what it means."

"That's what you've been so worried about?" he asked. "You should have told me." Galen crossed his arms over his chest, cocked his head to one side and narrowed his gaze. "But there's something else, isn't there?"

I grimaced and nodded; my eyes downcast. "Before we left the summit the wolves from Alaska stopped by our cabin. They're from a *demon* wolf pack and they said that my mother was one of them..." my breath caught in my throat, but I purged the poison which had been haunting me from my veins. "Which would make me one of them, too."

His gaze dipped down to the spot on my arm where I'd been marked by a demon; seemingly coming to the same conclusion I had. That the demon attacks on the Long Claw pack had some-thing to do with me. And suddenly the few feet that separated us felt like a canyon. We were on opposite sides and there was no bridge to cross the distance. The silence between us built into a deafening roar as I waited desperately for him to say or do something—anything.

Galen had asked for the truth, and I'd given it to him. What came next was up to him. All I could do was hope for the best, but I would have been a fool not to mentally prepare myself for the worst.

Rejection.

My heart ached and my whole world shrunk down to this one moment. No matter what happened now, I'd spoken my truth, I'd found my courage... I'd kept my word. And now I was at the mercy of my Alpha and my mate.

·CHAPTER 6

GALEN

Be careful what you wish for. You just might get it.

I'd begged, pleaded, and threatened Talia just to get her to tell me the truth. Now that she had, I was faced with an entirely new problem I had no solution for. And I had no fucking idea where to even begin to try and find one...

Talia had been marked by a demon shortly after the attacks began. I'd known that the demon mark meant *something*, but I assumed Talia being the one that was marked was a mere coincidence. An unfortunate twist of fate at best. A demon had appeared in my father's house and attacked. She'd bravely fought back, and the bastard creature had marked her. That was the end of the story, or so I thought.

But Talia being the *cause* of it all? Talia being the reason a demon appeared at my dad's home, that the witches had been cursed, and my pack members murdered? The thought had never crossed my mind. Until this moment. My stomach roiled and my heart thumped in my chest as some of the puzzle pieces finally began to fall into place.

But what did she mean—a demon wolf pack? Were they

mixed blood, both shifter and demon at the same time? Was that even possible? And was Talia a harbinger of doom? A curse on our very town and pack? Had I damned the pack to destruction when I made her a Long Claw? When I *claimed* her as my mate?

None of that matters.

The only question that was worth asking was how was I going to save her? Because losing her was not an option. I'd fallen head over heels in love with her. She was my mate. Not just my mate, my fated mate. Mark or no mark. It didn't bloody well matter *what* she was. I knew *who* she was in her heart, and I would do whatever was necessary to keep her by my side. I knew how I felt before the words even formed in my mind.

"Your eyes... do they turn red every time you shift?" I asked as I uncrossed my arms and hooked my thumbs in my pockets; switching up my body language and hoping I appeared more relaxed. But the truth of the matter was that I was far from it. I needed to see her eyes for myself, and there was a good chance Talia would close herself off and run when I asked her to show me. It would be the final testament of the strength of our bond. "I need you to shift, Talia."

"Here?" She whipped her head around, her golden-red locks fanning out around her as she searched the room behind her. "What if someone sees me? If they find out what I am, they'll want me thrown out of the pack... And you're their Alpha. You'd have to do what is right for the pack."

"You're what's right for me, Talia, and that makes it right for the pack." I closed the distance between us, pulled her into my arms and reassured her with a kiss. "Everyone left. Even Theo, Marcus, and David are gone. We're alone, but I'll lock the doors if it will make you feel more secure. You can trust me. You know that, right, baby?" At least, I hoped she did.

"So, you're not rejecting me?" she asked, her heart in her throat as she gazed up at me with hopeful and plaintive eyes.

"Of course not!" I clutched her tighter. After the way I'd acted back at my apartment, I couldn't blame her if her faith in me had faltered. I'd taken her secrecy as a personal slight and that whatever she was hiding from me was somehow about me or about us. And in a way I supposed it still was because her problems would always be mine to bear, too.

Talia feared rejection, which was understandable after everything she'd been through. She was afraid of losing me and the pack—of being marked by a demon and tossed out to fend for herself in a world that had shown her nothing but cruelty and pain.

"I claimed you, Talia. No demon mark, demon wolf pack, or you having red eyes is going to ever change that. We're going to fix this. Just don't shut me out anymore, okay? We'll fight this, whatever it is, together."

Talia's eyes filled with tears, but her lips quirked up in a smile. Quickly, she stripped out of her clothes, tugged on our bond and the magic inherent in all shifters, and shifted into her wolf without any further fear or hesitation. Her change came faster and with less effort or signs of physical pain than I'd expected. Obviously, her demon blood aided in her change, helping her not only shift, but recover from the strain of it.

"It's going to take a lot more than red eyes to mar the beautiful wolf standing in front of me," I said with a smile of my own. I'd seen Talia's wolf on a number of occasions and red eyes didn't change my opinion of her or her wolf one damn bit.

She circled in front of me a couple of times, then curled up at my feet.

I squatted and ran my fingers through her thick, midnight black coat from tip to tail.

"You need to stretch your legs and go for a run, don't you?" I thought back to the last time Talia, and I, had been on a hunt together. "It's been a while, hasn't it? How about I drive us out to the perimeter checkpoint, and you can run the woods while I stalk the property line? No one will bother you out there."

Talia turned those big, round eyes on me, pulling me into their endless ruby depths. All of the obstacles she'd had to face, that we'd had to face together, only made me love her that much more. She was my warrior wolf and gave my life new meaning.

She opened her mouth, tongue lolling to the side as she panted her approval of my plan. She really was an incredibly striking wolf—her ruby-red eyes simply added to her already unique beauty.

"Afterwards, we'll swing by the apartment and pack a few things. We should come back here to stay, I think. I can't ask the pack to hunker down on the property and not do the same." I stroked Talia's fur and scratched behind her ears. "We'll stay at my dad's place."

Talia turned her head, bathed my palm with her tongue, and nuzzled closer against my shins. She knew I'd avoided going home ever since the funeral and just how much staying at the ranch home would cost me personally. But if I wanted to lead, I needed to lead by example, even if it meant dealing with the pain of my father's loss head-on by living in his home; surrounded by his scent and memories.

"All right." I gave her one last scratch behind her ears and gathered up her clothes before heading out to my truck parked around the back. "We better get going. I want to make sure you're in the woods before the watch shift changes."

I dropped Talia off at the tree line, waited until she disappeared under the cover of the evergreens and shifted into my own wolf. To my relief there were no signs or smells of any demons while I was on patrol.

The hour spent running the length of the western border passed without incident. I checked in with Talia through the pack bond, ensuring she hadn't run into any trouble before covering the half mile between the property line and the massive pit that opened up in the ground during the last demon attack.

Marguerite and the coven had already worked tirelessly to close the canyon but a crack large enough for a horde of unholy creatures to climb out of, still scarred the pasture. Sarah had assured me that wards would be put in place to seal off the demons' entry point before the night was out, but I wanted to check their progress before I left for town.

The once tall, green grass was charred and black. Sulfur and smoke overpowered the smell of the wild clover and heather that dotted the landscape, and the field resembled a dystopian nightmare. It would take years for the area to recover, if it could recover at all.

When I arrived the witches had formed a circle around the large, jagged opening and stood with their arms outstretched, heads back, chanting to the moon. Small tremors could be felt underfoot as they called on the goddess to aid them and channel their magic.

Satisfied the coven had things under control, I doubled back in search of Talia. Her energy in the pack bond changed, which meant her physical form had as well.

"Everything okay?" Talia popped up from her stretched out position in the back of my truck, slid to the edge of the bed and dangled her legs over the tailgate. "I was starting to worry that something had happened to you." She was forced to wait for my answer until after I shifted but seemed relieved by my presence all the same.

"Everything is as good as can be expected," I assured her as I strolled to the front of the truck, enjoying the way she ogled my naked body when I walked past her. "The coven was almost finished casting the spell to seal off the demon pit when I left them."

"It's a good thing your trade-off with Marguerite for staying on the property is proving beneficial still. If they were in town, they might not have been here before another demon made its way through. If they came at all."

"You don't think they would have helped us if they weren't staying on the property?" I asked, her comment surprising me.

My father and Marguerite had a working alliance based on a stipend for years. While I no longer had the coven on retainer, it hadn't occurred to me that she would have said no if we were truly in need. Of course, Talia was right, though. Even if she had chosen to honor the allegiance, the coven's residences were too far away for them to have come to our aid during the battle.

"Oh, she would have helped you," Talia answered. "But at what cost? I don't think the pack could afford it." She offered a lopsided grin and shrugged. "But I don't think you'll have to worry about that when this is all over. You've earned each other's loyalty now."

I grunted in agreement, grabbed my clothes stacked on the driver's seat and got dressed while Talia's words rang in my ears. Had I done enough to earn Marguerite's loyalty? And if not, at what price could she be bought by an enemy of the Long Claw pack? It was a disturbing thought.

Between the demons and the pack battles, our numbers were a fraction of what they were a year prior, but I refused to raise dues on the pack. Our business ventures and investment holdings were tied to the local economy and suffered right along with us thanks in part to the demon attacks.

The pack's finances were on the same downward spiral as our luck. But luck could change with the wind and I had a feeling ours was about to turn. Though, that feeling could have had something to do with the violet-blue eyes beaming at me from the back of my truck. No matter how bad things were, I felt like anything was possible with Talia at my side.

If push came to shove, I would sell the bar to pay for Marguerite's loyalty to the Long Claw pack. However, for the time being the coven and the pack's missions were aligned and we had an agreement that worked for both of us. Stop the demons and stay alive. But Talia and I had another mission altogether. One that didn't involve the coven or the Long Claw pack. At least that's what I hoped.

We needed to know more about who and what Talia was. Her red eyes, the wolves from the demon pack that had approached her at the summit and what they'd told her... It had to mean *something*. We just needed to find out what that something was. And I finally had an idea about how to find out.

"I think we should go have a little chat with your aunt." I started the truck and turned on the heat on low, just enough to take the damp chill out of the air.

"I reached out to her after my expulsion from the pack, and she agreed to let me stay with her after Dad died, but she's been estranged from the family for years." Talia drummed her fingers against her thigh and tapped her foot against the floorboard of the truck. "I doubt she knows anything. She's been out of the loop too long."

"I'm willing to bet she does and that's exactly why she hasn't spoken to your family in years." I shifted the truck into reverse and backed out of the parking lot.

"It's possible, I guess," Talia said as she stared out the window lost in her thoughts.

Not that I blamed her. She had a lot to process. We both did. "I think it's more than possible. It's probable." I pressed my foot on the gas, increasing my miles per hour to almost double the posted speed limit, and drove back to my father's house.

"It's only a few more blocks to the ranch." Talia protested, gripping the dash with one hand and the console with the other. "I think you can slow down now."

"Sorry." I eased off the accelerator and dropped my speed to a more respectable nine miles over the limit. "It's just, we're running out of time and after the last attack... I hate to leave the pack."

"I get it, I do. The sooner we leave, the sooner we get back." Talia rested her hand on my forearm and squeezed. "But we can't figure anything out if we die in a car accident."

"Yeah, that would slow things down a bit." I spared a glance in her direction and gave her a playful wink.

"Just a bit." She used her index finger and thumb to indicate a small unit of measurement with a roll of her eyes.

"Pack whatever warm clothes you have," I instructed as I pulled into the driveway and shifted into park.

Talia was out of the cab and in the house before the truck's engine had even stopped running. I followed her inside, pausing at the door before shaking off the sudden melancholy thinking of my father, and we made short work of packing a couple bags for the trip north to her aunt's homestead.

We tossed the suitcases in the bed of the truck, agreed on what details were essential and which we were worth omitting, and then met up with my Betas back at the bar to explain the situation.

Someone's got to be in charge in my absence.

"I hate to leave you guys again so soon," I offered by way of an apology to all three of them.

They'd pulled more than their share of responsibilities in the weeks prior and even more so after my father's death when I didn't have the capacity to handle anything outside of mourning him.

Talia and I stuck to our agreed-upon story and left out the part about her red eyes and a possible missing princess that may or may not have been her mother. Instead, we said that it was Talia's aunt Victor and Victoria had mentioned at the summit, along with a demon wolf pack who lived in Alaska somewhere near the Arctic Circle.

"Demon pack?" Marcus narrowed his gaze, zeroing in on Talia. "Our town is a hot spot for attacks. Is there a connection to her family?"

"Maybe that's why she was marked?" David lowered his gaze to the tip of the scar on Talia's forearm where it peeked out from under her sleeve.

The mark was another item we agreed to fully disclose to my Betas. I hated the thought of keeping them in the dark about anything, but I promised Talia not to share what happened when she shifted with anyone until after we'd met with her aunt. We needed more information.

As expected, their reaction to the news of a demon pack alone confirmed Talia's fears of causing a panic if they were to learn the whole truth. I'd convinced myself the secrecy was for the good of the pack and my Betas' peace of mind. Only time would tell if I was right.

· CHAPTER 7

TALIA

G alen kept his word and my secret. I hated asking him to lie for me—even if it was by omission—but he agreed that the pack wasn't ready to hear about my direct connection to a demon wolf pack or my red eyes. Not after they'd just lost so many of their loved ones. They'd no doubt come to the same conclusion Galen, himself, had and if that were the case... they might want blood.

Grief was a hard cross to bear, I knew that all too well. And though I'd done nothing to actively harm the Long Claws it seemed my mere presence had stirred the depths of Hell itself. So, I wasn't sure if I could blame them if that's how they felt. From every conceivable point of view, it sure looked like I was.

Galen left Marcus, David, and Theo in charge. Again. Yet another thing that I could have been held responsible for. As their new Alpha, Galen had delegated more responsibilities to his Betas since I had arrived.

I wondered if they ever regretted going along with Galen's ridiculous plan to kidnap me for leverage against my Ex in the first place, but I was too afraid to ask. The truth often hurt and that was another reason why we had decided to keep details to a minimum—at least until we got back from our trip to Kansas. Without information we were as good as unarmed, and our foes were relentless.

Approximately two hundred miles of green and gold corn field separated us from my aunt. It had been years since I saw her last, and months since I'd called her in tears and all but begged for her help. Yet, now, we were less than half a day's drive from her doorstep with no more than a voicemail left to announce our impending arrival.

"If she answers the door, it'll be a miracle." I dug my phone out of my bag and scrolled through my contacts for her number. "Maybe I should call her again?"

"The sun is barely up, Talia." Galen reached over and rubbed his hand along my forearm to comfort me. "I doubt she's even out of bed yet," he reasoned. "If she still hasn't gotten back to you by the time we hit Wichita, we'll make a pit stop somewhere and try to call her again."

"I could use a pit stop now, actually." I pointed to the reflective blue sign on the side of the road that advertised a few gas stations and fast-food restaurants.

Galen topped up the tank and ducked into the adjoining convenience store for a few snacks to tide us over.

In the meantime, I hit the restroom and ran a brush through my long red-gold hair. Scrutinizing my reflection in the scratched-up mirror, I found myself truly grateful my ruby eyes didn't show through while I was in human form or it would be back to wearing dark sunglasses no matter the weather; because there was no way we could let non-shifters learn about our existence, let alone real demons.

That would endanger us all.

"All good?" Galen asked when I joined him at the checkout counter. He dropped the coins from his change into a pet shelter collection cup on the countertop, grabbed a plastic bag filled with a variety of sweet and salty snack options and another with bottled water.

"As it will ever be." I sighed, and reached for a cardboard drink carrier with what I assumed from the invigorating scent were two cups of fresh coffee.

"It's going to be all right, Talia. Your aunt was willing to take you in when the shit hit the fan. There's no good reason she wouldn't be willing to tell you about your family now, when you're in need of the information." Galen merged back onto the highway, navigating the traffic until we maneuvered the truck into the lane we needed.

I could think of several reasons my aunt wouldn't want to delve into our family history or divulge secrets about any demon pack roots we had, but I kept them to myself. There wasn't any point in hashing them out. She would either talk to us or she wouldn't, and we were about to find out which...

As Galen had predicted, my aunt called back once it was a more reasonable hour and she'd had her morning coffee. She was expecting us and to my surprise, sounded genuinely happy that we were paying her a visit.

I doubted she would feel the same way when we left. She'd no doubt managed to live a safe and quiet life away from the danger that stalked my mother to her grave, and now we were bringing the proverbial storm to her doorstep.

The four-lane highway eventually dwindled to two before dropping down to a single-laned dirt road with cheery sunflower fields on either side. A strip of grass covered the hump in the center of the road which was worn down over time by God-only-knew how many tractor tires.

A white-washed two-story farmhouse with a rust-riddled tin roof and a lopsided front porch lingered in the distance. The old, black-metal mailbox at the end of the drive leaned to one side of the wooden post it was fastened to and its door hung open on one hinge. The whole homestead looked like I felt—a little weathered and worn, but still holding on for dear life.

Aunt Sylvia waited on the porch for us wrapped in a faded and pilled terry cloth blue bathrobe, the belt cinched tight around her narrow waist, waving as we pulled up and parked on a patch of gravel raked out along the side of the house.

She pressed one hand to her mouth and the other over her heart and watched me climb the splintered, wooden porch steps with misty eyes. "Let me get a good look at you." She held me at arms' length, her fingers encircling my wrists. "You remind me so much of your mother. You have her eyes."

Just a few weeks before I would have preened at the compliment. It had been *so* long since my mother passed, my memories of the way she looked had begun to fade away by the time I reached my teens. But faced with the possibility of a demonic wolf pack lineage, it was hard to take that comparison as a compliment at the moment.

"Now, who's this handsome man you've brought with you?" Aunt Sylvia released my wrists and turned her attention to Galen. "I thought you broke off the engagement?"

"I did. Well, he did," I corrected as my face warmed and no doubt turned a light shade of red as I pointed at Galen. "I mean, he didn't. This isn't my Ex."

"I'm Galen, Alpha of the Long Claw pack." He climbed the porch steps and introduced himself, saving me from my embarrassment.

"You're a little more than that," my aunt observed as she looked between us, before motioning for him to come closer. "Let me get a look at you too." She raked her gaze over his body, from head to toe.

"You're awful young to be an Alpha. And the Long Claw pack you say? What happened to the old Alpha, Max?"

"My father recently passed, I'm afraid." Galen did his best to hide the pain in his voice, but I heard it, and I assumed my aunt could, too.

She'd known Max. Perhaps she'd have a story to tell about him as well as my mother and Galen could find solace in our journey too?

"You could do worse than a Long Claw." Aunt Sylvia winked at me and wrapped her arm around my shoulders, steering me toward the front door. "Another Alpha, huh?"

"It doesn't matter if Galen is an Alpha or not. I didn't plan it that way." Unsure of whether that was a good thing or a bad thing, I hedged my answer. "It just sort of happened."

"Of course, you didn't, dear. These things are never planned. They're always destined." My aunt ushered me into her living room, sat me down on a worn-out black leather sofa and motioned for Galen to join me. She plopped down into a matching recliner. The tanning on the arms had faded away to a light gray and there was a patchwork quilt draped over the back of the chair, giving the space a very lived in and homely atmosphere.

"So, fate brought you two together," she said as she watched me.

I wiggled free of my jacket and folded it in my lap, chewing on my lower lip.

Her gaze fixed on my arm. "Just not in the way I expected. That's not the mark of a fated mate on your forearm, Talia, but something else entirely."

"You know what it is?" I blurted, unable to contain myself now that answers were apparently so close at hand. I'd planned to ease my way into the conversation about demon eyes and the mark one demon had left on my arm, but I'd been absent-minded when I'd removed my coat.

"Oh yes, I know more about demon marks than I care to admit, and if your mother were alive today, so would you." Aunt

Sylvia planted the soles of her feet against the floorboard and pushed to get the recliner rocking.

"Her mother? You're sure it wasn't something to do with her father instead?" Galen asked. He must have seen the surprise in my eyes at his question because he reached over and rested his hand on my knee in a show of quiet support. "Your father was killed by his own pack, babe. It seemed like a valid question."

"Because it is a valid question," I said, reassuring him despite needing a little reassurance myself. The validity of his question didn't make the circumstances of my father's death hurt any less. Though ties to a demon would have been a better reason for permanent exile or death, than simply not following orders.

"No, it was definitely your mother." Aunt Sylvia eased back into the chair, pulled the wooden lever on the side to raise the footrest and stretched out her legs.

"How can you be certain? I mean, how well did you know my dad? Mom died when I was little, and I don't remember you while I was growing up..." I winced at my choice of words and hoped she didn't think I was being rude or accusatory about her absence. We'd come for information and we wouldn't get any if I started off by offending her.

"Your mother and I shared more than a last name, Talia." She offered a weak smile that did little to hide the pain in her stormy blue eyes. "The question you should be asking isn't how well I knew your father, but how much do you really know about your mother?"

"I don't. I know practically nothing. I tried over the years to get my father to tell me something, *anything* about her, but he dodged my questions like the plague and drank himself into a stupor whenever I brought up her name."

Galen turned his hand palm up, offering his support once again.

I gratefully took it, entwining my fingers with his.

"Well, the truth is that you're not Northwood pack—not really—you never were." Aunt Sylvia closed her eyes and released a heavy sigh. "Neither were your parents. Either one of them."

"But my dad *was* a member of the Northwood pack," I interjected. "He raised me as a member, too." I shook my head, not able to make sense of what she'd just said. "You must be wrong."

She has to be.

My days with the Northwood pack were well and truly over. My membership had been revoked and I'd been exiled, but that didn't erase my upbringing or my father's lineage. Unless that was yet another lie. I sighed. There were just so many. The ones I'd told Galen, the ones Maddox told me, and it seemed my father had told his fair share as well. It was impossible to keep track of them all.

"I take it he never told you the story of how they met?" She sucked a breath between her teeth and pursed her lips. "I'm not surprised."

"But you know...?" I ventured; my brows creased.

"There were no secrets between your mother and I, but it just so happened I was there at the time." Aunt Sylvia raised her hand to stave off any more questions or interruptions. "Your father was a rogue and he lived on the outskirts of our village long ago."

I almost laughed at the impossibility of it. "You expect me to believe my father was a lone wolf?" I scoffed, unable to hold back given the absurd picture she painted. "He could barely take care of himself! He needed the pack and was as loyal as a golden retriever to the very end."

"Some might say your mother tamed your father, or that she broke his spirit, but neither is true. She soothed something truly wild, something very dark and deep within him. In fact, if I had to use one word to describe their relationship, it would be *fierce*. They were a force to be reckoned with when they were together."

Aunt Sylvia stopped rocking and leaned forward; the metal mechanism packing as she forced the footrest closed.

"You said your father couldn't take care of himself... Did you ever stop to wonder why? And don't say because he was an alcoholic." She pointed her index finger at me, pinning me to my seat with her gaze. "That was a symptom, not the problem. Your mother had demons of her own—real ones—and your father fought them! He protected her like a loyal warrior. And he didn't like to talk about the things he'd seen because he'd seen some truly scary shit."

Galen sat in silence, transfixed by every word my aunt spoke as my parents' story unfolded before us.

It certainly wasn't the story I'd expected. I'm not sure why I thought it would have gone differently for my parents. When I looked back on my childhood, there weren't very many sunny days, or rainbows. The silver linings were few and far between for our little family.

I was well cared for, and my father loved me. I had no doubt about that, and I never wanted for necessities, but there was a perpetual cloud that hung over us. A dark storm that had settled over our house the day my mother died, and it followed us wherever we went like a curse—a reminder of what we'd lost—a fog of sadness that rolled in and clung to everything.

It seemed like things had finally taken a turn when I reached my teens. My father continued to rise up the pack's ranks, and I had a job in town. Not long after that I'd caught the eye of the Alpha's son. We were fated it was said, and I was going to get the happily ever after my parents never had. Maddox and I were going to lead the pack, have children, and grow old together. I thought we were in love...

But nothing turned out like I'd planned. Not that I was complaining, now—at least when it came to being mated I'd dodged a bullet there. The jury was definitely out when it came to my demon pack lineage, but something told me that whatever my aunt had to say, it wasn't going to be good. But regardless of what I was about to learn, I'd swallow it down, accept it, and find a way to deal with it and move forward. I had to; for me, for Galen, and the Long Claws.

"After all these years, why now?" Aunt Sylvia's hands trembled in her lap. "Why are you really here, Talia, asking all these questions?"

"You already know why, don't you?" Galen barked out a bitter laugh, fell back against the couch cushions, and rested his right ankle over his left knee. "Talia's visit isn't a surprise. I can sense that much. You knew she was coming, with or without her father's passing, you were just biding your time until she showed up. You knew she would."

"Galen!" I chastised, raising my hands in a placating gesture to my aunt who'd jumped to her feet at his accusation.

The conversation had just taken a hard left turn. I had no idea where Galen was steering it, and it didn't look like it was getting back on track any time soon.

"I knew. Of course, I knew!" she answered. Aunt Sylvia's eyes flashed a familiar shade of red; her wolf zeroing in on me like a frightened rabbit when I gasped. She squinted her lids shut and shook her head, forcing the beast within her to settle back down. "But I had hoped it skipped a generation. It has been known to happen in our line. My parents, your grandparents, they belonged to the same demon pack, but their eyes never changed. And with you only being *half* demon wolf, I thought it even less likely you'd inherit the trait."

"So, you thought it would be better for me to just figure it all out on my own?" I stood up and closed the distance between us. "What is the point of family if all they do is lie to you?"

"Whatever you're looking for, it needs to stop here." Aunt

Sylvia gripped my shoulders, her fingernails digging into my arms with a frightening intensity.

"Galen and I came here looking for a way to stop the demons attacking our town and to find out how I'm connected to them."

"I'm so sorry, Talia. There's nothing I can do about the mark. I don't even think the Alpha could help you."

The Alpha. Galen? Or is she referring to someone else?

She tightened her grip on my arms, her nails piercing my skin through my thin cotton shirt. "If the demons are attacking, it's already too late... for all of us."

"What Alpha?" Galen pressed, pulling her off me and giving her a gentle shake to snap her out of her hysteria. "Sylvia, what Alpha?"

Galen knew most of the Alphas in North America on a first name basis. If there was even a remote chance that this mysterious Alpha, whoever he was, could help us, we had to take it. Otherwise, my aunt was right, and it *would* be too late.

· CHAPTER 8 ·
GALEN

Talia's aunt had known about Talia's hereditary condition the whole time. She'd hidden away from the world on her homestead in Kansas and hoped that the demon scourge that plagued the rest of the packs wouldn't land on her doorstep. But they had—the moment her niece arrived.

I pressed her for more information on the demon packs and where we could find them. We soon learned the Alpha she had been referring to was none other than the leader of their family's demonic pack. Without question I knew, if the demon pack wolf Alpha was our last shot at stopping the attacks and finding a way to remove Talia's mark, we had to try and find him.

Once we'd gathered the information we needed, Talia and I hit the road again. This time we headed north, across the Canadian border and then west to Alaska. Three thousand five hundred and twenty-four miles stretched between us and our destination.

But who's counting anyway?

Me, that was who. With everything going on back home this was a race against the clock and as we faced three days of nonstop driving, time was most definitely not on our side.

To get there as fast as possible, we made the trip in shifts—one behind the wheel and one asleep in the passenger seat. The truck did not stop unless the fuel light came on, and even then, it was only temporarily. We'd find the nearest gas station or truck stop with a twenty-four-hour convenience store, grab what we needed and hit the road once more.

Talia would stock up on drinks and snacks to fuel our bodies, while I filled the tank and then we'd be off again; covering as many miles at top end as my V-8 could before we ran her dry and she needed refueling again.

When we swapped roles for the next leg of the journey Talia passed out the second she'd buckled herself into the passenger seat and rested her weary head against the window. She was exhausted, mentally and physically, but it wasn't just from driving sunup to sundown. Visiting her aunt had really taken a toll on her. The reunion hadn't been at all what Talia had expected.

Hell, I hadn't seen shit that coming either.

Talia's family, on her mother's side, were demon pack wolves with red eyes. Though Sylvia's were a paler shade than Talia's, I'd noticed. I wasn't sure if it was just a physical trait like having dark or light brown eyes, or whether it meant something more——something insidious. So, I'd filed that tidbit of information away for later. It was on my long list of concerns I planned to ask the demon pack Alpha—if and when we found them.

Soft trails of yellow-green punched through the absolute darkness of the Anchorage skyline. The city slept, unaware of the horde from hell hot on our heels and working their way across the continent.

I'd never met a demon wolf before Talia, and she'd never known she was one. Not until the mark on her forearm activated something inside her, and her aunt had gone on to confirm it with their family's history. But all the same, my gut told me that there was *a lot* more to the story. Her aunt was leaving something out, something she didn't want us to know, and I had every intention of finding out exactly what that was.

No matter how I diced it, I couldn't shake the feeling that Talia was in danger and that I was the one driving her straight toward it. "Talia, we're here." I nudged her arm softly. "Come on, babe, wake up. We made it to Anchorage."

She stirred momentarily, mumbled something about turning up the heat, and curled herself up into a ball on the seat once more. The position she was in looked uncomfortable as hell, but she didn't seem to mind and slept through every bump and bounce when I veered off the main road and onto a gravel drive that led to a small private airport. Our next stop was a remote town outside of Prudhoe Bay, and only accessible by aircraft.

I pulled into a parking space alongside the hangar and left Talia asleep in the cab of the truck while I went in search of our pilot. The plane was on the tarmac and our bags were loaded by the time she woke up.

The pilot taxied down the runway, prepared for takeoff and made the ascent without incident.

Sylvia's information got us as far as Prudhoe Bay, but the rest was up to us. The demon wolf pack was settled somewhere above the Arctic Circle and lived their lives in sub-zero temperatures, surviving harsh conditions that left them isolated from the rest of the world. I wasn't expecting a warm welcome, not just because of the reading on the thermometer.

"Thanks for letting me sleep," said Talia as she adjusted her headset and swiveled the mic up into position near her mouth. "I'm sorry you had to drive the last leg on your own. I was just so tired."

"You don't have to thank me. I was too wired to sleep anyway, and I know you're exhausted."

Talia had grown increasingly fatigued over the past few

months. Her energy levels had first started dropping when the demon marked her, and she had been on a steady decline ever since. It didn't bode well, and I was more than a little worried about her.

The pilot's voice came over our headsets with a warning about turbulence.

Talia gripped my hand, her knuckles white as she squeezed my fingers like a vice.

The plane rocked and shook, jarring left and right as it fought the extreme weather. The pilot pushed forward on the yoke of the plane, pointing the nose of the aircraft and the propeller down to descend, attempting to get under the changing air currents.

"Oh my... I mean, holy shit..." Talia struggled with a string of expletives, one hand pressed firmly to her chest, the other still clutching mine in a death grip. "That felt like an earthquake."

"Yeah, except five thousand feet up in the air!" The pilot's laughter cut in and out over our headsets. "But we've passed the Talkeetna Mountains. So, it should be smooth sailing from here on out. First time flying, huh?" he asked.

"Is it that obvious?" Talia's laughter reminded me of wind-chimes jangling at the mercy of her frazzled nerves, rather singing with the breeze. She released my hand and wiped the sweat from her palms on her jeans. "I'm sorry."

"That's a bad habit, and one I'm going to have to break you of eventually." I stretched my hand and shook off the feeling of pins-and-needles in my fingers.

"What do you mean?" Talia sat up straight in her seat and blinked in surprise, her violet-sapphire eyes showing confusion. "What did I do?"

"You apologized... again," I explained with a wink and a lopsided grin. "You do it *all* the time, even when you have nothing to apologize for."

"Old habits die hard, I guess." Her meager smile and heavy

sigh confirmed my suspicions—that she'd accepted the blame for everything and had been made to apologize for things that were never her fault in the first place all her life, simply to remain in the Northwood pack's good graces.

"You will never have to say you're sorry for being yourself with me," I promised as I cupped her face in my hands and leaned in, pressing my lips to hers in a tender kiss. "Never again. That life is behind you."

"Right behind me," Talia sighed, resting her head on my shoulder and nuzzling into the crook of my neck. The warmth of her breath raised goosebumps across my skin. "And just how do you plan to break me of this terrible habit, exactly?"

"I have my ways," I hinted suggestively as I ran my hand along the inseam of her jeans to the top of her thigh. "You'll be saying *please*, instead of sorry."

"Is that so?" she whispered into my ear, before nipping my lobe between her canines.

"Oh, it's a promise." I slid my hand over her hip and cupped her ass. "The next time I hear you say those words..."

"I'm sorry, Galen," Talia teased, her voice raw with need. She opened the bond between us, drowning me in a wave of emotion and flooding my senses.

I could hear her desire in her hitched breath and racing heart; smell and taste it in the air. She drove me—and my wolf—wild without even trying. But we wouldn't be joining the mile-high club. At least not on this flight. Privacy was not a feature of the Kodiak we'd chartered to fly us into Prudhoe. It was something I hadn't considered when I initially made our travel arrangements. As it was, the pilot could hear everything we were saying to one another, but I tried not to focus on that awkward detail.

The mountains soon gave way and the landscape changed before our eyes, from peaks and valleys to a flat frozen tundra that looked uninhabitable, let alone capable of sustaining and hiding a demon wolf pack.

"Attention passengers, if you look out your windows you will see the Dalton Highway and the town of Deadhorse." The pilot informed us over the radio. "I've turned on the fasten-your-seat-belt light. We'll be making our final descent into Prudhoe Bay in just a few minutes."

As promised, our pilot landed the plane shortly after his announcement and taxied down a runway dusted with snow that would have caused most pilots to ground their planes and cancel their flights—but for him, it was just another Tuesday—which made me immensely grateful I'd hired him.

Talia and I bundled up against the cold, slipping on insulated hats and fleece lined gloves. We even hiked the collars of our thermal winter coats higher in an attempt to block the blasts of cold air from reaching the sensitive exposed skin of our necks. Hopefully, we blended in with the locals. But something told me we were overdressed compared to the few residents bustling about who'd long ago acclimatized to the bitter winds and temperatures here.

We left the airstrip, luggage in tow and headed into the small town which consisted of two hotels—possessing the only eateries available—and just enough infrastructure to support the oil workers who called Prudhoe home.

"Welcome to Days End Hotel." The concierge greeted us before the automated doors had even closed behind us. "Checking in?"

"Yes, we have an online reservation. It's under Linetti." Talia hitched her backpack up on her shoulder and crossed the spotless, white commercial tiled floor.

"Ahh, yes. Miss Linetti." The concierge flicked his gaze between Talia and the bulky, outdated monitor connected to the desktop computer whirring beneath the counter. "I regret to inform you that we're actually all booked up for the season."

"What? But that's impossible. I booked a room on your website three days ago." Talia's bag slid down her arm and fell to the floor beside her feet. She rested her elbows on the counter, peering over the concierge's side to catch a glimpse of the information displayed across his screen. "Check it again," she said firmly.

"I assure you, Miss Linetti. I've checked it twice." The concierge ran his finger between the collar of his uniform cinched around his oversized neck and tugged at the navy-blue woolen fabric. "There must have been a glitch in the system. It should not have allowed another booking. I am sorry."

"I've been in a car for days and dealt with ass-numbing turbulence on a ridiculously tiny plane. I haven't showered, slept in a bed, or had a meal that wasn't prepacked and overpriced from the snack aisle of a convenience store. And now you're going to tell me I don't have a reservation because of a glitch?" she growled, her elongated nails tapping menacingly against the countertop. "There's going to be a glitch in *your* system if you don't figure out what the hell—"

"What my overtired and under-fed girlfriend is trying to say, is that we would really appreciate your help given our situation." I reached into my back pocket for my wallet, pulled out a few twenties and slid them across the counter. It was all the cash I had on me, but if the upturned nose and disdainful look in the concierge's eyes was any indication to go by, we were going to need more than eighty dollars to grease his chubby palms.

"Certainly, sir. I'd be happy to assist you." The concierge replied, sarcasm dripping from each word as he swiped the bills off the counter. His fingers flew across the keyboard, keys clacking as he punched information into the system. "Yeah, I'm sorry," he drawled, his tone lacking his previous professionalism. "Looks like we're still fully booked. Why don't you try the hotel across the street?"

"Well, that was eighty bucks well spent," I muttered, before snatching Talia's backpack off the floor and steering her through the lobby and back out the door into the arctic winds.

"I cannot believe this!" A cloud of condensation carried Talia's frustrations with it into the swirling atmosphere. "I booked the fucking room. They debited my account for a nonrefundable deposit."

"We both know that wasn't a glitch." I glanced over my shoulder at the concierge, warm and comfortable behind his desk, in the midst of an animated phone call. "They don't want us here."

"Obviously," she huffed, inching her scarf up over her ears. "What are the odds that the only other hotel in this god-forsaken town has a vacancy?"

"Is that a rhetorical question?" I hooked my arm through hers and stepped off the curb. "But let's go find out."

We braved the cold and trudged across the icy street, only to be met with more of the same.

Something is going on here.

"The Best Days Inn did *not* live up to its name," Talia hisses as she huddled over the hot cup of complimentary coffee she'd helped herself to while we'd waited for yet another concierge to deny us a room.

"Nope. It did not." I brought my hands to my mouth, exhaled a breath of warm air over them and rubbed them together to keep the blood flowing into my extremities. "They knew we were coming and are hell bent on making sure we don't stay here."

"Do you think the demon pack is behind this? Victor and Valerie seemed pretty interested in getting to know me. So, why go through all the trouble of stalking me at the summit just to shun me when I came all this way?"

Why indeed?

Talia's question was a valid one—and I didn't have an answer for her. But she was right, it didn't make any sense. The only two demon wolves in attendance at the summit had purposely sought her out. They were the ones who set us on this path—in search of more information about Talia and the pack she belonged to by birth and by blood. They knew we'd follow the breadcrumb trail...

"I think we better start by tracking down your friends. Come on." I grabbed our luggage and started the trek back toward the airstrip. "Let's see if our pilot is still here. Maybe we can catch a lift back to Deadhorse."

Someone in Prudhoe Bay had gone to a lot of trouble to run us off—and they'd succeeded. At least for the time being. Together, we retreated to Doulton's Dead End and the town of Deadhorse to regroup. But we'd be back. We came all this damn way for information, and we weren't leaving until we got it.

CHAPTER 9
TALIA

The residents of Deadhorse were just as tight lipped as their neighbors in Prudhoe, but at least they were more hospitable. We found an available room in a boarding house and bar that had been a part of the town since its founding in the seventies. The room had a draft, the water was tepid, and the bar was dry.

I'd hoped for a hot bath, followed by a hot toddy, but settled for a hot chocolate and a hot-blooded Alpha on the brink of losing his temper. "We'll catch more flies with honey," I said as I sipped the steaming liquid chocolate and licked the whipped cream mustache from my upper lip.

"This coming from the woman who damn near went over the front desk to get her claws on a concierge?" Galen glanced at his phone and checked the time. "Not even two hours ago."

"That's fair." I chuckled and nudged him with my shoulder, careful not to spill any of the drink in my hands. "Want to order another round?"

"Are you hoping that if we keep ordering four-dollar mugs of hot chocolate the woman behind the bar will be compelled to spill her guts and tell us everything she knows about a pack of demon wolves roaming Alaska's frozen tundra?"

"When you put it that way, it sounds like a ridiculous plan." I winked at him over the rim of my mug. "But it's the best plan we have. We're off grid, out of allies, and almost out of time. It's the people in this bar or bust."

"Marshmallows or whipped cream?" Galen asked, his hand already in the air to signal the bartender, who doubled as our waitress.

"Marshmallows, please," I answered.

Our server returned with our drinks and set fresh mugs in front of us, cautioning us that they were piping hot. "So, it's pretty obvious the two of you aren't from around here. Or even Alaska, for that matter," she said. The leggy brunette cocked a denim clad hip to one side and tucked her black plastic tray under her arm. The green and brown flannel she wore brought out the flecks of yellow in her eyes.

Wolf.

I kicked Galen's shin under the table to get his attention without making it obvious to our waitress. How had she managed to hide her scent from us? If not for the specks of yellow in her iris, I never would have suspected a thing. It looked like we could add spy to her list of job duties at the Dead End boarding house.

"So, what brings you to Deadhorse?" She smacked on a piece of gum before stretching it over her tongue and blowing a small bubble. "You with the pipeline or something? The boys and I have a bet going. My money's on corporate."

She jerked her thumb in the direction of a table on the opposite side of the room. Three men, ranging in age and size, shared a pitcher of what I assumed was cola and two baskets of hot fries.

"Really, why do you say that?" Galen reached for his mug and brought the steaming hot chocolate to his lips.

"Jake's betting on you two being tourists, given your expensive taste in cold weather gear. But I figure, if you can afford those coats, you can afford a tropical vacation." She pulled the tray from under her arm and loaded it with our empty mugs.

"Was there a third guess?" I unwrapped the utensils from the paper napkin and used the spoon to scoop up a couple marshmallows from my mug.

"Lincoln thinks you're here looking for something." She narrowed her gaze, fixed it on me and leaned in close, the tray precariously balanced on her palm. "For your sake, I hope he's wrong."

"What if we are looking for something?" Galen clasped his mug in both hands and leaned back in the wooden chair, his legs stretched out in front of him and crossed at the ankles.

"You know what they say about curiosity," she said as she set the loaded tray on an empty table to her right.

"I guess it's a good thing I'm not a cat, then." Galen appeared casual and aloof, but I'd learned the small muscle ticks and twitches that were tells of his aggression bubbling just under the surface.

"Neither are we." She glanced back at the table occupied by Lincoln and his friends, all of whom were now on their feet.

"We didn't come here looking for trouble," I assured her, raising my hands in a placating gesture as I tried to diffuse the situation.

"That's too bad, pretty lady." One of the locals stepped out from behind the table, cracking his knuckles on each hand. "It looks like trouble found you and your friend anyway."

All three men were itching for a fight. They crossed the bar, one on point and two ready to flank us from both sides.

I recognized their moves. Maddox and his Betas performed drills on small pack hunts and practiced fighting techniques all the time. Though that information wasn't as helpful as I'd hoped.

We were outnumbered four to two. Galen was more than capable of handling himself in a fight and despite my lack of training, I'd done the same against the demons attacking our town on more than one occasion.

But we've never fought together.

We needed to move as a unit, play on each other's strengths and offset our weaknesses. Still, we had one advantage. A trick up our sleeve that our attackers shouldn't have been able to detect.

Our bond.

The connection between us deepened beyond what was typical of an Alpha and a member of his pack. It was yet another confirmation that Galen, not Maddox, had been the mate fate had chosen for me.

"We're going to have to fight our way out of here." Galen's voice rubbed against the inside of my skull like velvet against my skin, soft and decadent, but there was an undercurrent of something else. Something I wasn't used to hearing in my mate's voice in the face of a fight—an edge of concern.

"Galen? What is it?" I asked through the bond, fighting against the nervous energy that circulated between us.

"They're armed with more than just their claws and fangs." His warning, which he'd spoken aloud, came just before the man our waitress identified as Lincoln drew a gun from his waistband.

"Right you are, and I'll give you one guess as to what they're loaded with." Lincoln sneered, a glint of light reflecting off his gold capped incisors. His other teeth had been filed to points and added to his menacing look and danger as an opponent.

We were a long way from home with no allies, limited resources, and were about to fight for the first-time side-by-side. The odds were stacked against us, but we still had our own edge.

Galen reached out through the bond, sharing his thoughts with me before he conceded to Lincoln. "Well, gentleman, it looks like we've got ourselves a good old-fashioned stand-off." Galen uncrossed his legs and sat up straight; wood cracking as his hands gripped the arms of the chair.

Click, click, click.

Lincoln and his friends cocked their revolvers and steadied their aim.

"I don't think you understand the situation at all, friend." Lincoln turned his head to one side and focused on me. "But you do, don't you honey? You can see this isn't any old revolver. You know what it is?" He twisted his wrist, rocking the gun back and forth a little. "This one's an Alaskan special, named after us because we hunt big game. This little Ruger snub nose will take down a bear. Now, imagine what it will do to a wolf when it's loaded with silver bullets." Lincoln's upper lip curled up at one corner, and he sucked in air between his teeth.

"I think she's getting the picture now, Lincoln." The waitress snickered, fished a cell phone out from the pouch pocket on the faded green apron tied around her waist, punched in a number and brought it up to her ear. "Hey, John, yeah, it's Lydia... Got it. The boys will bring them in...Yep, they're on their way." Lydia pointed at Lincoln and his lackeys, and then to us. Her scowl and rough, aggressive motions seemed to indicate the person on the other end of the phone wasn't happy and was in a hurry to meet us.

"Let's go." Lincoln jerked his head in the direction of the door. "And don't even bother trying to make a run for it. If I don't kill you, the weather will."

Galen and I communicated through our bond, agreeing to do as we were told until the right opportunity presented itself for us to escape. We still needed answers to the questions we had about the demons and my family's connection to them, but that information was useless to us and the Long Claws if we were dead.

The men led us out of the restaurant and boarding house to an SUV parked in the alley along the left side of the building.

"Turn around and face the truck." Lincoln lashed nylon rope around our wrists, bound our hands, and then covered our heads with dingy, grease-stained cloth sacks from inside his vehicle.

We were shoved roughly into the rear tray of the SUV. The arctic cold penetrated the steel frame of the truck, seeped through my clothes and settled into my very bones. The accelerated metabolism that caused a shifter's abnormal body temperature was useless in subzero temperatures. It couldn't compensate for that level of cold. My teeth chattered hard enough to chip a molar and caused a searing pain in my lower jaw.

Three doors slammed shut, the engine fired up, and radio blared a skull rattling base through the speaker system in the cargo hold. The throttle revved and held steady at a high RPM for several minutes before the vehicle took off.

Ice and snow crunched under the tires as the SUV rumbled over the frozen ground for what felt like hours. My shoulders burned, threatening to pop free of their sockets as I struggled with my bonds and worked my arms beneath me, sliding my legs through. Galen did the same and we worked to loosen the ropes on each other's wrists enough to provide relief and better circulation, and inched up our hoods to see, but stopped short of freeing each other.

Instead, we laid there, the short, abrasive automotive carpet fibers rubbing the small of my back where my coat rode up and contemplated our next move. Lincoln was right. We could run, but we had nowhere to go. With no heat, shelter, or food, death in the arctic was imminent. We could free ourselves and go in for a surprise attack, fighting Lincoln and his lackeys in close quarters increased our odds.

It also increases our odds of an accident.

And then we would be in the same situation as if we'd made a break for it. Sure, the truck would provide some shelter but only if it sustained minimal damage and if it was in working order, and the heat only lasted as long as the gas in the tank did. For the time being we were at their mercy, but it seemed crystal clear that the first pack of wolves we'd crossed paths with in Alaska was less than compassionate.

We only had one option, and that was to play our capture out. Galen seemed to think that we were being taken to a camp or compound that belonged to the pack and I agreed. They were bound to have supplies stockpiled on site. So, we'd take what we needed and get the hell out of there the first chance we were afforded. The demon wolf pack was still out there somewhere, and we had to find them. Our pack, our town, and even our alliance with the witches depended on us.

Finally, we heard Lincoln bark orders to his underlings and eased the truck to a stop.

Galen and I scrambled to tighten the knots on our bonds and secure our makeshift hoods before they came around to the back of the SUV and pulled us out of the tray.

"I thought I told you to tie their hands behind their back." One of the men shouted, followed by a meaty thump.

"Oomph. I did!" Another grunted. "What the hell, Wylan?"

"Well, why are their hands in front of them then, Jake?"

Wylan must have whacked his partner, Jake, again because it sounded like a fight broke out behind the SUV.

"Knock it off! A storm's moving in and it's fucking cold out here. Grab them and get them inside before we all freeze our asses off." Lincoln barked at his small crew and got them back in line.

I was by no means a fan of our captor, but he and I saw eye to eye with him on at least one thing—it was fucking cold.

Bitter winds whipped through the cargo area as Lincoln's wolves rushed to follow his orders. Every inch of my exposed skin felt like it was jabbed with a thousand tiny needles. Tears leaked out of the corners of my eyes and left frozen, crystalline tracks running down my cheeks.

The storm had thrown a wrench in both our plans it seemed. Ultimately, we had no choice but to wait it out and take advantage of our captors' shelter before making our escape—but no matter what happened we were determined to get out of here.

Alive.

CHAPTER 10
GALEN

Despite the harsh reality of our situation, Talia maintained a brave face.

In return, I did the same for her. But neither of us were fooling the other. Our bond had been wide open since we first encountered Lincoln and his buddies in the bar, which meant so were our feelings. Everything was laid bare between us, and neither of us could hide it, even if we wanted to.

She was afraid—of the unknown, of what might become of us, of what could befall our loved ones and pack if we didn't succeed.

So was I. In a way, I hoped she took comfort in that, in knowing that it was okay to be scared and that I didn't think less of her—or think she was weak. Any wolf who saw my mate as weak was making a huge mistake. She'd survived grief, rejection, banishment, demon attacks, and a demon mark. She was stronger than anyone gave her credit for.

Including herself.

Lincoln and his idiot henchmen led us by gunpoint from the SUV into a massive encampment that consisted of dozens of prefab buildings common to research facilities in remote loca-

tions. The site was remote but based on the number of inhabitants it felt anything but temporary.

They pushed us to the front of our party and walked us
through the center of the pack's makeshift town. Blinds and
curtains were cracked as its inhabitants peered out their windows
for a glimpse of the commotion outside.

The front door of a metal framed building that resembled the
shape of a tunnel with weather resistant fabric stretched over its
arches, opened up. A large man with ruddy skin and a white beard
struggled against the wind to hold onto the door. "Take them
straight to the pens." He cupped his mitted hand beside his
mouth and shouted over the howling wind.

"Pens?" Talia's thoughts echoed my own through the bond.

*"It's going to be all right. Whatever happens, we're going to get
through it together. I'm right here with you."* I did my best to reassure
her, sending all the love I felt for my mate through the bond.

"Come on, move it!" Lincoln jammed the barrel of his pistol
into my back and nudged me forward. "Make a left between those
two buildings over there."

Talia and I trudged along a snow packed path between the
two buildings. The sounds of barking dogs drowned out the rattle
of the wind battering the metal structures of all sides.

"You two mangy dogs ought to fit right in." Lincoln chuckled,
stepped in front of us and pounded three times on the door.

The door cracked open and a raven-haired kid that looked to
be no more than fifteen poked his head out. He took one look at
the party gathered outside and scurried back inside the building.

"Finish feeding the sled dogs and get your ass back home. This
should have been finished an hour ago. Your mother will be
looking for you." Lincoln forced his way through the door,
yanking me behind him.

"I was just prepping the fish for the morning," the boy stammered, slipping on his puffy coat and outer weather gear.

"Good, now get the hell out of here and keep your mouth shut about these two, you understand? I don't need you worrying your mother over two rogues." Lincoln grabbed the kid by his collar, and heaved him toward the door, before letting him free.

The kid opened the door and disappeared into the swirl of snow beyond.

It occurred to me then that Lincoln assumed we were rogues. I'd made the same assumption about them. I'd thought that they were a ragtag pack of misfit wolves with no real lineage or Alpha.

That was an error in judgment on my part and theirs.

The smells of urine, feces, and rotting fish were sucked up in a back draft of air when the door opened and closed. The putrid combination was like a sucker punch to my olfactory senses and a jump starter to my gag reflex. Saliva built in my mouth, and my stomach convulsed, but I held down the ridiculous amount of hot chocolate I'd had back in Deadhorse out of sheer spite. I would not look weak in front of our captors.

I'm an Alpha. Be an Alpha, Galen.

Talia looked green around the gills as well. She swallowed hard a few times, her body jerking as she fought through a violent bout of nausea.

"There're a couple open crates in the back. Lock them up. Bryant will deal with them in the morning," Lincoln instructed, pulling a blue and white bandana from his coat pocket to cover his nose. "I hate coming in here. It fucking reeks. You two finish up and meet at my place when you're done."

An ear-piercing chorus of dog barks and howls erupted when we entered the kennel.

Waylon and Jake led us down an aisle with metal crates on either side to the empty boxes against the far wall.

The mix of huskies and malamutes paced circles inside crates just large enough for them to stand at their full height inside. The barking increased in fervor and decibel as the two men forced us toward our cages. Cages that were not meant for humans—or at least, shifters in their human form—but I had a feeling we were not the first shifters to occupy these holding cells.

"Get your hands off me!" Talia spat at Jake's feet and jerked her arm free of his grip. "I don't need your help." She dropped to her knees and crawled inside the crate without further argument.

"Looks like you've got experience on your knees." Jake snickered, elbowing his friend in the side. "That's good. It'll make things easier for you when you meet the Alpha. He likes his women nice and subservient."

"I'm impressed, Jake." Talia took advantage of Jake's momentary confusion and kicked him in the shin, landing a physical parting shot along with her verbal one. "I wouldn't have guessed you even knew what that word meant."

"Bitch." Jake kicked the door of her crate and punched a few numbers into the keypad secured to the right panel of the metal box.

"You're not going to cause trouble now, are you?" Waylon grabbed a cattle prod hanging from a hook on the back wall and pointed it menacingly at me.

Rather than waste my strength in a fight with two shifters and four thousand volts of electricity, I followed Talia's lead and dropped to my knees, crawling into the cage.

"That's what I thought." Jake kicked the door shut and punched in the lock's code. "Welcome to Boot Hill, assholes," he said. "Where hell is literally frozen over."

Jake followed Waylon out of the kennels, running the barrel of his gun along the bars of the crates as he went to rile up the dogs and then slammed the door closed behind him.

"Talia, are you okay?" It was a stupid question and one I knew the answer to already, but I asked it anyway. Neither of us were okay. The whole situation was *not* okay and had been screwed up since the moment we set foot in Alaska.

"Yeah, how about you?" She wrapped her fingers around the small bars of the small windowpane and peered out across the aisle at me.

"It's not the best place I've ever stayed, but it's not the worst either. The service leaves a lot to be desired. I'd give it two stars," I joked, hoping to lighten the mood and our spirits. Though that was easier said than done, given the incessant barking and stomach-churning, concentrated ammonia smell.

"If I could leave zero stars, I would!" Talia laughed and her violet-blue eyes sparkled from behind the bars. "Two stars, really? That's generous."

"It's good to hear you laugh," I said with a sigh. It was like music to my ears on the best of days, but on my worst, it was akin to an epic and beautiful symphony.

"There's no use crying over spilled milk or pending death." Talia's red-blonde hair brushed the bars as she shook her head. "Besides, crying never solved anything—trust me—I speak from experience."

"Laugh or cry, huh?" I reached through the bond and used the magic ingrained in all Alphas to soothe our wolves. "I thought we'd moved past bottling things up?"

"Oh, don't worry. A good, long cry bordering on full blown breakdown is coming, but I am saving it for when this nightmare is over. I'm no good to either of us if I fall to pieces, now," she reasoned. Talia was so much stronger than she knew and it only made me fall harder for her every second of every day.

"Note to self, go to the wholesale store and buy a bulk package of tissues. Got it." I sucked in a deep breath and let it out slowly, preparing myself for the shift in our conversation. I wanted to keep things light, but it was time to get serious and come up with a plan.

"Talia, at some point one or more of the wolves in this pack are going to come back in here. When they do, we need to keep our cool, listen to their conversations and gather as much information as we can. Like, how many of them there are; what if any supplies they have easily accessible. Do they have any wheels we can steal, like snowmobiles or a Snow Cat, okay?"

"They remind me of my old pack to be honest. Maddox and his ilk would have paraded us in front of his father by now. I ignored so many red flags... ugh. Ignorance is bliss, right?" She blew out a heavy breath and sighed. "Anyway, if they're anything like the Northwood pack, they'll be coming in here sooner rather than later and we'll get an audience with the ranking officials. We should pay attention to the pecking order and find the weakest link in the pack."

"The kid who feeds the dogs, Lincoln's boy? He might be a good place to start." My lip curled back, and my canines elongated, pressing against my bottom lip, when I recalled the way he'd treated his son.

"Maybe..." Talia seemed to chew on my suggestion for a moment. "But he's just as likely to go the other way and rat us out due to a fear of repercussions. You saw how rough Lincoln was."

"Yeah, you might be right, but—"

"You're going to try anyway." Talia's smile came to life in her voice and through the bond. "You want to save him too."

"If I can." I answered as I rested my head against the steel bars. I still felt the sting of losing my father and watching the young teenager recoil from his father struck a personal chord and stirred my Alpha's primal instinct to protect. "I know it's crazy... I don't even know the kid. Maybe it's because we just buried my father? Hell, I don't know, maybe it's—"

"It's because you're a good man, Galen. There doesn't need to be any other reason than that." Talia stretched and reached through the bars, straining her fingers. The aisle was too wide for us to touch each other, even when I tried too, but it had had the comforting effect she'd clearly hoped for.

"We should try and get some rest if we can," I suggested, clearing my throat of the emotion that clogged it up. "We're going to need our strength for what lies ahead."

The sound of metal slamming against metal jolted me wide awake. I'd just dozed off when a couple of wolves returned to collect us. The only wolves we'd been introduced to, or at least knew by name, were nowhere to be seen.

Six wolves dressed in knock-off U.S. military style extreme cold camo gear, complete with a digitized disruptive pattern of white with gray tones, marched down the aisle and split off into two groups of three in front of our cages. One from each team operated the keypad on the locking mechanism and entered the codes.

I focused on the tones, engaging my sensitive shifter hearing and listened for the slightest variation and memorized the sequence. If I could get my hands on some sort of stick or rod, I could try to match the tones to the numbers on the pad. From there, I could unlock the door and get Talia the hell out of Alaska the first chance I got. It wouldn't solve the demon pack mystery, but our jaunt out into the frozen wilds had put my mate's life at risk and I'd remedy that before anything else.

"Let's go. Get a move on." The leader on each team barked orders at Talia and I, shoving us forward when we tried to stretch out our cramped muscles.

We hadn't been in the cages long, but it was enough to put a crick in my neck, back, and every joint in my body. I would have given almost anything to shift and insta-heal myself of the niggling pains.

They marched us out into the cold, back through the alleyway we'd come when we first arrived, and out into the center of the encampment where a large group of wolves had gathered around a ring of fifty-five-gallon drums filled with split wood.

The silver haired, white-bearded Santa Claus who'd ordered

us to be kept in the kennels stepped out of the crowd and poured off-road diesel onto a chunk of wood. Red drops of fuel fell onto the snow, staining it a strange pink as it seeped its way down to the earth below. He lit the accelerant-soaked kindling with a cigar torch lighter and tossed it into one of the barrels. A blast of warm air whooshed out from the barrels as the fumes from the gas-soaked logs packed inside them ignited one after the other.

"My name is Bjorn," he announced. "Alpha of the Deofol pack." He raised his arms above his head and the crowd behind him roared. He gestured for his wolves to settle down and continued with his introduction. "We don't get many visitors to the town of Boot Hill, at least not uninvited ones. I'm sure you can understand our need for caution."

The audience laughed and threw slurs and jeers at us, the unwelcome and unwanted outsiders.

I scoured the crowd for any sign of empathy on the faces of the Deofol pack members but found none. But something else besides kindness was missing in the group gathered around us—the kid from the kennel, Lincoln's boy.

My wolf stirred, worry and anger churned within me, but I tamped them out before the dangerous combination caused me to combust. If something had happened to him, I would make sure the person responsible paid and suffered in kind.

"It might surprise a couple of soft, city dwellers like your-selves to know that we have 5G this far north, but lucky for you we do." Bjorn turned away from us and gave his attention to the wolves at his back. "Brothers and sisters, I gathered you here in the town square for a celebration, not a public execution. At long last one of our missing wolves has finally come home."

The Alpha spun around, his silver hair fanning out around him, and pointed squarely at Talia. "Welcome, Sister Linetti." Bjorn roared as he stretched his arms high above his head.

The crowd echoed his words, welcoming Talia back to the pack.

"Galen," Talia gasped, a hundred words unspoken in the one breath of air expelled from her lungs.

Was this the pack we'd been searching for and had hoped to gain information from to use against the demons back home and save Talia from the demon mark? The same pack it turns out who'd just threatened to kill us and held us captive in deplorable conditions. They were nothing like the wolves we'd met at the summit.

I couldn't help but wonder if Valerie and Victor weren't from a different demon pack altogether. Maybe we hadn't found the one we were looking for after all, but some dangerous, extremist offshoot instead. But that was the least of our problems, which said a hell of a lot about the situation in which we'd found ourselves.

The Deofol Pack Alpha had done his research and publicly claimed Talia as one of their own. He knew something we didn't. And whatever it was, it did not bode well for either of us. Again, we had no choice but to see how this all played out.

Fuck.

CHAPTER II

TALIA

They say the road to hell is paved with good intentions, but it's also paved with fucking snow. Our hosts, or captors, depending on which side of the bonfire you were standing on, turned out to be the very demon pack Galen and I had been searching for it seemed.

Aunt Sylvia had warned us against seeking them out and perhaps this was why. We'd willfully ignored her and forged ahead with the Long Claw pack, the coven, and our town's best interests at heart. We wanted to save those we loved... and walked into the fire. But now, having come face-to-face with my demonic extended family, I wish we had listened. They were nothing like I'd hoped and far worse than even my aunt feared.

Things have gone from bad to worse in record time.

Bjorn had publicly introduced me to the pack as a lost sister. He'd done some homework while Galen and I were locked up in the kennel with their sled dogs; and it seemed the information he found online confirmed what Valerie and Victor told me at the summit—I was a demon wolf.

Part of me had hoped that they were lying, and that my aunt

had been mistaken about our lineage. The other more naive part of me had hoped for a happy reunion, that I'd have a family again, and that they'd help us stop the demons attacking us. But neither of those things happened.

"Talia, your mother left us and chose to start a new life and family with a rogue wolf outside of the Deofol pack. She paid her debt in blood, and we hold no ill will toward you." Bjorn called out a man named Colson and beckoned him forward. "In fact, Brother Colson welcomes you into the Bone Pack with open arms. Come forward, sister, and embrace your family."

"No." I raised my hands and backed away. "I have a pack now. I don't care what you found out about me or what my blood relations are to any of you. I'm Long Claw by choice and by heart."

"You can't deny your blood, Talia." Bjorn laughed off my declaration and marched forward, closing the distance between us.

Galen stepped boldly in front of me but was rushed by two of the guards who had retrieved us from the kennel originally. They dragged him away as he fought tooth and claw.

"You've been marked. I can feel it through our pack bond." Bjorn pushed his way into my mind, clawing violently at the connection I shared with Galen until only a tattered thread remained between me and the Long Claw pack.

I collapsed, dropping to my knees under the weight of his voice and the force of his intrusion inside my head.

"Talia!" Galen called as he struggled against the shifters who'd pinned him to the ground. "Don't touch her," he roared. "Get your fucking hands off her or I will break every bone in your body!"

"Tough talk from a guy face down on the ice." One of the guards reared back and landed several kicks to Galen's ribs and unguarded face.

Galen coughed up blood, dotting the stark white snow with crimson spots, but he never stopped fighting to break free.

"You better get more men, Bjorn, because if I get loose, I will end you." Galen spat out another mouthful of blood, straight onto the boot of the wolf who'd assaulted him.

"Is that a challenge from the Long Claw pack that I hear?" Bjorn sneered, a silver capped incisor poking out from behind his curled lips.

My mate fell silent, and his body stilled beneath the guards holding him. The next words he spoke were spoken only for me through our bond. His voice was a comforting caress for my soul even if what he said broke my heart.

"I'm sorry, Talia. I can't challenge him. Not now." Galen's personal torment leaked through the bond before he shut it down and closed me off completely.

I gasped aloud. The silence was deafening. I hadn't realized just how much space he'd occupied in my heart and mind until he locked himself away from me.

I understood why Galen had made the choice he did. I'd been groomed to be the wife of an Alpha all my life and while Galen couldn't be more different than Maddox, his duty was still to his pack fire and foremost. He couldn't risk them for anything, not even his mate, and I wouldn't expect or ask him to. A sentiment I would have gladly shared with him if he hadn't gone radio silent.

"I didn't think so." The Alpha knew Galen wouldn't formally challenge for the Deofol pack. He'd won the standoff without a drop of his own blood spilled. And without anyone left to stop him, Bjorn was free to proceed with his show of dominance. "Look!" he commanded as he grabbed the hem on the back of my coat and yanked it up over my head, exposing my bare flesh to the freezing cold. "She's been chosen. She bears the mark. There is no denying it."

I cried out from the physical and mental anguish of yet another public violation and humiliation.

A second mark? On my back?

My mind reeled.

As if one wasn't bad enough.

I thought back, scouring my memories for a time when the second mark could have happened and came up empty. Which meant the demon had marked me a second time and I hadn't even realized it—and that terrified me.

"Fate has chosen Talia, the Bone Pack princess, as the demon's mate." Bjorn clasped Colson on the shoulder, congratulating him and the other pack members for the blessing bestowed upon them.

"Blessing?" I screamed at the top of my lungs. "This isn't a blessing. It's a goddamned curse. I'm cursed!"

"My dear child." Colson knelt down before me and pinched my chin between his forefinger and thumb; pressing harder when I tried to jerk away. "Our demon wolf god has chosen you as his mate, and as such a great honor has been bestowed upon the House of Bones."

"Since when are demons honorable?" I spat with disdain clear in every word. "Do you even care about the destruction happening outside your borders?" It hadn't escaped my notice that the only place left untouched by the demon hordes that were running loose in wolf territories all over the country were the towns associated with the Deofol pack and their attached packs.

"Of the four houses, the Bone Pack was chosen. The demon wolf god looked upon us with favor despite your mother's betrayal." Colson tightened his hold on my chin to the point of bruising. "You will accept this mating or suffer the consequences as she did."

"Did you kill my mother?" I growled, clasping my hand around his wrist and digging my partially shifted claws into his skin until I felt the warmth of his blood well up around my fingertips.

"She chose her fate," Colson said as he risked permanent damage to his veins, before he yanked his hand free of my grip. The skin damaged from my razor-sharp nails had already begun to scab over. "Karma came for her."

"You will graciously accept the demon wolf god's proposal and sit at his side as his mate, or you will reject him and kneel at his feet forever as his concubine," said Bjorn as he stepped in front of me, his fur lined, tan suede snow boots obscuring my field of vision. "Either way, he will claim what is rightfully his."

"I would rather die than accept his proposal," I snarled. "I am no bitch to be claimed! I am already spoken for. I have chosen my mate!"

"As much as it would pain your brothers and sisters to witness your death and have shame cast upon their house again, that could be an amicable solution." Bjorn ripped my knit hat from my head and grabbed a fistful of hair. His nails dug into my scalp as he forced me to look up and meet his gaze. "That would free you of your physical obligations, of course, but he'd still lay claim to your *soul*."

Bjorn tossed me aside roughly, sending me sprawling sideways into the snow and strolled back to the circle of burning barrels to warm his hands over the flames. "Whatever you decide, the demon wolf god will have you. He always gets what he wants." The Alpha wrung his hands over the fire, soaking in the heat as flames licked his skin.

"Not this time." I snarled again, letting my fury fuel me and pushed myself to my feet.

"Talia, wait. Don't back him or yourself into a corner," Galen said aloud, before continuing privately through our weakened bond. *"Please, let's think this through. We'll come up with something together. We just need time."*

"Your lover clings to hope. It is a fool's hope, but I have to agree with him." Bjorn broke through our connection, terrorizing my most private thoughts and the safe place I'd found with Galen. "You don't want me as your enemy, and you really should give this some serious thought. Rash decisions so rarely pan out—just ask your mother. Oh, that's right, you can't. What a pity. I'm sure she would see things the demon wolf god's way if given another chance."

"You son of a bitch!" I growled, unable to control my wolf any longer. The change came hard and fast. Bones cracked, skin split, and fur sprouted. Every inch of me burned with a rage so hot it threatened to consume every cell in my body alive. The Deofol wolves had admitted to killing my mother and had just sentenced me to a fate worse than death. My wolf demanded vengeance and she wasn't taking no for an answer.

A hush fell over the demon wolf packs clustered around the burning barrels. They gawked, eyes wide and mouths agape like fish out of water, cooking beneath a blazing summer sun.

My wolf, covered head to toe in a coarse midnight black coat, stared back at them with her piercing ruby-red demon eyes. I recognized the bewildered look in their expressions. I'd been just as struck by my new appearance as they were. Except my reaction had been born of horror and not of awe or reverence.

"She carries the trait! More proof that she is the next Bone Pack princess and our lord's fated mate." Bjorn thrust his index finger in my face but jerked his hand back before my gnashing teeth snapped around it.

A low growl vibrated up from the darkest depths within me and out of my mouth. I gave myself over to my wolf and she took the reins without hesitation. Hackles raised, she lunged for Bjorn and her teeth found their mark, clamping down on his leg.

Without hesitation he dropped a hammer fist down on the top of our skull.

Black spots danced around the corners of our vision, but we didn't let go, instead we sank our teeth deeper into his calf. The coppery taste of his blood coated our tongue, fueling my wolf's need for vengeance by way of violence.

Bjorn grabbed us by the scruff of our neck, tearing our incisors through his own muscle and sinew as he yanked us off him. He shifted into his wolf as soon as our jaws let him go. He was a massive hulking beast with a coat the same shade and texture as mine.

The sounds of another fight breaking out behind me reached my ears. Galen howled. Whether from pain or rage I couldn't tell, but I didn't dare take my eyes off my opponent to find out. I put my trust in Galen's wolf to keep him safe.

The Deofol Alpha fought with the ease and experience of a wolf that had earned his place at the top of the pack. He circled, stalking his prey, waiting for my inexperience to provide the perfect opportunity. And when the opportunity presented itself, he seized it. No matter how hard I fought, Bjorn eventually found an opening and bit down on the underside of my neck, ratcheting his jaws closed until he blocked off my air supply and I was forced to submit.

I was outmaneuvered and outmatched.

His shift back to his human form was as quick and effortless as the one to his wolf. And from the relaxed look of his pack members, he did it without pulling on their bond at all. He didn't need to borrow from the pool of their power, which spoke volumes about just how strong he was.

"Maybe a night in the box will change her mind. Take them back to the kennel." Bjorn barked orders at the security team and checked himself for any injuries that might not have fully healed during his transformations to and from wolf.

Some distance behind me, Galen lay in a battered heap.

One of the guards fastened a leash around his neck like he was a common mutt and dragged him over the snow and back to the kennel. while

I limped along beside him still in my wolf form, another guard at my side and a Ruger aimed squarely at my head.

They tossed us in our crates, locked the doors and switched off the lights, leaving us to suffer in darkness and stench.

I reached out to Galen through what little remained of our bond, but he didn't respond. His breathing was labored but I took comfort in the fact that he was still breathing at all. He needed time for his wounds to heal. So, I left him in peace and curled up in my cage to lick my own wounds—metaphorically and physically speaking.

As my crappy luck would have it, it turned out Valerie was right.

My mother *was* the lost Bone Pack princess. She had obviously rejected the demon wolf god's claim and in doing so, her pack. No wonder she had run as fast and as far as she could from Alaska.

She had probably believed fate was on her side when she'd crossed paths with my father and had the opportunity to join the Northwood pack. But nothing could have been further from the truth. Fate sided with the gods—one in particular—and all my mother had done was pass her rejected destiny onto me.

CHAPTER 12
GALEN

I woke naked and sore, covered in crusted blood, and back in a cage inside the kennels. Red flakes cracked and peeled off my skin, coating the concrete floor around me in evidence of my pain. It was still dark. The sun's restorative rays hadn't yet penetrated the cracks and crevices in the kennel that had been overlooked in its construction. Wind whistled through the gaps, largely invisible to the naked eye.

The sled dogs slept through the previous night's activities without complaint. There were almost times that I envied wolves with only one form. Ruled by their basic needs and survival instincts, they weren't bound by greed or hate, or evil and selfish desires for power. They simply hunted, slept, and reproduced. They survived.

Talia's wolf was a survivor too. She stood up for herself—for us—and fought like hell against Bjorn and the Deofol pack.

I had been terrified at first that the Alpha would kill her for her disobedience. He reminded me a lot of the Northwood Alpha in his irrational and unforgiving behaviors. Except Bjorn was worse.

97

Much worse.

Alaska and the Arctic Circle had proven to be a wild, harsh frontier beyond my wildest imaginings, and the wolves who lived here adapted to it. They were as hard and cold as the ice their town was built on... and they were evil.

They knew the demons were attacking our packs, our towns, and that people were dying. And they didn't care at all that innocent blood was being spilled. They worshiped a demon wolf god and basked in his benevolence while the rest of the world burned.

No wonder Talia's mother ran away and never looked back.

I couldn't blame her for that and would have done the same if I were in her shoes, but I wished she'd had the chance to prepare her daughter for what was to come. I wished Talia's father hadn't been so utterly destroyed by her mother's death that he couldn't talk about who she really was. He had done his daughter a huge disservice in not sharing the details of her mother's heritage and what she had run from. Someone should have told Talia the monsters were real long ago... and that they were coming for her.

Talia's mother was the Bone Pack's lost princess and Talia was their new heir. A role she couldn't refuse, outrun, or hope to escape. It was abundantly clear that the demon wolf god wanted her for himself, and it didn't matter to him whether it was in this world or the next. But there was just one problem with that scenario—he couldn't fucking have her.

Talia is mine.

I fell in love with her the moment I saw her walking through town. The day she'd been cast out of the Northwood pack. The same day she was supposed to move to Wichita and never look back. How I'd never noticed her before that day was a mystery to me, but the threads of our fate had been entwined all along. We were orbiting around each other without ever knowing it, just waiting for the right cosmic moment for our paths to collide.

Talia was my Big Bang Theory. She didn't just create a new

world; she created a whole new universe for me, and she was at the center of it. She was my sun, with her golden-red hair and violet-sapphire eyes. I didn't need a mark to tell me that she was my mate. It was *fact* as far as I was concerned—an irrefutable truth. I knew she was meant for me; I felt it in my heart and my soul. And nothing or no one was going to come between us.

Not even a damned demon wolf god.

My wolf and I had failed yesterday. We'd fought a dozen wolves in the end when we'd kicked the two guards' asses, but were bested in the end, leaving Talia to defend herself against another pack Alpha. That would not happen again. We'd spent the night in a cage, licking our wounds and plotting our next move. The plan was simple: Save Talia and level anyone or *anything* that stood in our way.

We owe her that much.

"Galen?"

The melody of Talia's sweet voice entered my ears and soothed my soul as well as the savage beast that lived within me. At least, for the time being. "I'm here. I'm awake." I reached through the bars, wishing for nothing more than to feel her satin smooth skin and the warmth of her body against mine, instead of cold steel.

"Oh, thank Go... *goodness.*" Talia paused, swapping out one 'g' word for another, then laughed off the silliness of it. "No sense accidentally invoking anything, right?"

"With the way things have been going lately, I wouldn't be pushing my luck either." I chuckled, hating that there was even a shred of truth to that.

"I was so worried, Galen. I thought they were going to kill you last night." Talia fought back tears, but I heard them in her strangled voice. "I didn't realize there were so many on you until after I was forced to submit to Bjorn." She sighed.

"It's a price I would gladly pay for your freedom and our pack's safety," I said stoically. I needed her to know exactly where she stood with me. I needed her to know without a shadow of doubt, that her place was at my side. So, I dropped heavy emphasis on the word 'our'.

It's our pack and our future.

"Don't talk like that, Galen. I couldn't live with myself if something happened to you because of me." She clung to the bars and pressed her face against them. "You're locked in a cage, beaten to within an inch of your life because of *me*."

Her words stung my pride and broke my heart. She didn't need to carry that burden. As her mate and Alpha, I should have been the one protecting her. "I'm not here under duress, baby. I'm here because I chose to be here with you, to support you, and to help you find your family and finally be rid of the demon mark. That's what you do when you love someone, Talia. You put it all on the line for them—and I'd do it again. Even if faced with the same outcome, I'd still choose you. Every single time." My declaration seemed to strike a chord within her and unleashed the tears she'd held back so bravely only moments before.

"I hate that I can't hold you." I wrapped my hands around the metal bars, taking out my frustrations on the fabricated steel as I listened to her sob. The bars molded to the shape of my fingers as I tightened my grip. I pulled and pried in frustration. They bent but wouldn't break. Still, I refused to give up. I channeled my wolf's strength and continued weakening the metal until the first bar suddenly snapped free.

That's all I need.

The keypad was within arm's reach. I stretched my arm out of the expanded opening and fumbled around until I felt the digital buttons beneath my finger tips.

"Galen, what are you doing?" Talia peered through the bars of her cage, a glimmer of hope in her eyes as she watched my attempt to escape.

"What I should have done last night." I didn't elaborate, letting her believe I was talking about breaking out when in truth, I was referring to challenging Bjorn. One after another, I pressed the buttons, listening to the different tones and tried the combination from memory. It buzzed. "Shit."

Another failure.

It should have beeped.

"What if it has a silent alarm and you trigger it?" Talia said, begging me to stop. "Galen, please. You aren't at your best. What if one of the guards comes in? You'll get caught. Please, I'm begging you, don't make me watch them hurt you again."

"Don't ask me to watch them steal my mate and force her into an unholy union with a fucking demon god," I retorted as I continued to try my luck with the keypad. "I thought we might be able to reason with them somehow, but I was wrong. I won't sit in this cage, waiting for them to take you away. Not while there's still breath in my lungs and strength in my body."

I punched the keypad, mashing the numbers until I finally hit the right sequence and matched the tone to the one I'd heard yesterday. The lock beeped and clicked.

Success. Fuck, yeah!

The door swung open And I crawled out on my hands and knees. Pushing to my feet when I cleared the top of the crate, I stretched to my full height.

"Galen!" Talia gasped, her hands outstretched through the bars of her crate, beckoning me.

"Shush, it's all right. I'm going to get you out of here." My body felt electrified by her touch, recharging my belief even more that she was my mate. You don't feel that way about someone who is not the match to your heart and soul. It's not possible. There was only one logical explanation for how I felt about her, and that was that Talia was meant for me.

Mine, my wolf growled; eager as I was to free her from her crate.

I punched in the same sequence of numbers into the keypad on Talia's fetid prison but it didn't work. I tried again and again, but there was nothing but buzzing every time.

"Maybe there's a silent alarm," she stressed again. "Could they have changed the code remotely?" Talia squeezed through the bars and grabbed my wrist.

The main door to the kennels opened with a whoosh of arctic air, as if in answer to her question. Footsteps echoed in the entrance area and approached the inner door leading to the holding area. I kept at the lock, punching in random numbers at a fevered pace in desperation.

No, no, no!

"Hey, what the hell?" One of the guards charged into the holding room. "Jeff, get your ass in here. He's fucking loose!"

I abandoned the lock, turned on the guard and powered forward in a full sprint with my right shoulder pitched down like a defensive lineman making a play to sack a quarterback and hit him center mass. He went down hard on his back, and I stayed on top of him, hammering punches in rapid succession to his face.

He raised his forearm, blocking a few blows and tried to dismount me with a barrel roll to his side.

Grappling in the nude with a trained fighter proved dangerous for me and more than a little awkward for my opponent. Nudity was an inevitable part of our transformation as clothes never survived the shift. So, bashful just wasn't in our natures. The guard however, seemed to have a bigger problem with two-hundred-fifty pounds of naked man sitting on his torso than the punches that continued to land on his head. I used that to my advantage.

The second guard did not seem to share his partner's inhibitions. He burst into the room and jumped into the fray, grabbing me by the neck and forcing me to the ice-cold concrete. We wrestled on the floor, throwing body shots, upper cuts, and rapid punches to the back of each other's skull.

Striking on a moment of luck I rocked him with a knuckle punch to the temple that left him momentarily dazed and confused. The few precious seconds he sat stunned, teetering on the brink of a blackout, were all I needed to gain the upper hand. Or so I thought.

"Galen, watch out!" Talia's warning brought my attention back to the first guard, but it was too late.

Armed with one of the cattle prods, he rushed me and made contact with my ribs. The prod *zapped*, sending four-thousand volts of electricity arcing through my body. My size and pain tolerance were both well above average, but the stun gun was rated for an animal five times my size and there was no withstanding it.

I collapsed, my skin rubbed raw as I writhed on the concrete floor like a cut snake. Despite it being clear that I'd been incapacitated, the guard never let up on the trigger.

He ran the prod until it died and needed to be recharged.

Everything hurt, from the roots of my hair right down to my toenails. My muscles were contracting and contorting my body into heinously unnatural positions. I gritted my teeth against the pain and refused to cry out.

"Damn, Jeff. Did you see that?" The first guard twirled the cattle prod in his hand like a baton. "Woo. We battered and fried his ass like a piece of chicken."

"You idiot." Jeff, the second guard and evidently the brains of the duo, snatched the prod from his partner and tossed it across the room. "You almost killed him! Bjorn would have been *so* pissed. Not to mention, you could have fried me up right along with him."

They came over, one on each side and dragged me back toward my cell.

"I challenge Bjorn, Alpha of the Deofol pack, for control of the demon wolf packs!" I ground out between my clenched teeth, pushing past the pain with every ounce of strength I had left.

"You're either incredibly brave or incredibly stupid," said Jeff as he shoved me inside a vacant crate with a functional lock three down from my original one. "I'll pass along the message."

"No need." Bjorn waltzed into the kennels like he hadn't a care in the world. "I heard him loud and clear, boys."

"And?" I pressed him for an answer, hoping his pride and short temper would push him to make a rash decision—one that would be to my benefit. The effects of the cattle prod were already wearing off. One shift into my wolf form and I would be good as new.

But unfortunately for me, Bjorn wasn't a stupid man.

"I accept." The Alpha's smile said it all. He saw the play for what it was and counter maneuvered. "The challenge will take place in three days' time. And by the way, there are three demon wolf packs. Just so you know what you'll be fighting for, or rather, dying for."

"Three days? Are you worried you'll lose, Bjorn?" I asked, goading him into fight me sooner and swiped at the blood trickling from my left nostril with the back of my hand.

"I wouldn't want anyone to accuse me of taking advantage of an injured man and question the validity of the challenge." Bjorn flicked his gaze to Talia's cage and back to me. "Besides, we both know I am *well* within my rights to choose the date of the challenge."

He was right, of course, but I'd hoped to piss him off enough that he would have forgotten that particular rule.

"Be sure to shift. I want those wounds healed nicely before the challenge. I don't fight wounded wolves or lesser men. When you come to claim my throne, you better be ready and at your best, Long Claw." Bjorn strolled over to Talia's cage and dropped to one knee. "Good morning, Princess," he drawled. "I'm happy to see you weren't foolish enough to partake in this unpleasantness. A member of the Bone pack will be along to collect you shortly."

Bjorn stood, then, pivoted on one heel and marched over to his guards with promises of discipline to come and made his way out of the kennels with a parting shot at me. "You want to fight the inevitable, Long Claw? You think you're brave enough and strong enough to stop what's in motion? You go right ahead and take it up with our demon wolf god, personally and see just where that gets you."

Bjorn hadn't meant to, but he'd just given me an idea. An insane idea more likely to end in death than success, but I didn't care.

Talia is worth the risk.

It was high time the demon wolf god and I had a damned conversation.

CHAPTER 13
TALIA

J ust as Bjorn promised, members of the House of the Bone Pack came to retrieve me. But instead of armed guards, two women had been assigned as my escorts and arrived at the kennels with fresh clothes and a foil-wrapped plate of hot food.

Galen on the other hand had been served the same meal as the sled dogs, one bowl half filled with scraps and another filled with what passed for clean water.

I peeled back the aluminum foil, my mouth watering over the breakfast foods piled onto the plate and crammed a quarter of buttered toast into my mouth. I picked through the bacon, sausage links, and country ham, only eating half of the portion, reserving the rest for my mate.

"Thanks," I said as I padded across the kennel floor and shoved food through the narrow steel bars of Galen's cage.

"What are you doing?" One of the young women protested. She reached out but stopped short of touching me. "That food wasn't prepared for him!"

"Do I look like I care?" I handed Galen the last of the bacon and a hash brown patty.

"No, Your Highness, you do not," answered the older of the two women. She dipped her chin toward her chest and dropped into a half curtsey. "Please forgive Erin. It has been long since we've served royalty and she spoke out of turn."

Galen's wide-eyed expression mirrored my own.

"Don't call me that," I retorted in annoyance, rounding on the woman, who by my best guess was three times my age, and pointed my index finger at her. "I'm not *your* princess or anyone else's."

"My apologies, ma'am, but you *are* the Bone Pack heir whether you like it or not." She tucked an errant strand of her salt and pepper hair behind her ear. "You cannot deny the title."

"No?" I dropped the paper plate on the floor and charged toward her, stopping just short of getting up in her face. "Let's get something straight right here and now. I will never swear allegiance to your pack, and I am not binding myself to your demon god. My mate, the one *I* chose, is sitting right there!"

"This is blasphemy," the other woman, Erin, protested. She had ginger hair and a blotchy complexion and clutched her gloved hand to her chest as if she were about to swoon at the horror of my declaration. "If the Alpha were here—"

"I'd say everything I just did and more," I spat. I definitely had more than a few choice words for Bjorn and the rest of the Deofol pack.

"You bear the mark, Talia." The older woman, whose name I had yet to learn, tried to rationalize. "In fact, you bear not one, but two marks. This is clearly your preordained fate."

"Yeah, like I haven't heard that one before." I barked out a bitter laugh. "This isn't the first time a wolf claimed to be my fated mate. It's not even the second. So, this demon wolf god is going to have to get the fuck in line. Which, for the record, starts and ends with Galen."

"I don't understand why she was chosen, Maria. Just Look at her!" Erin looked to her packmate for support. "She doesn't deserve this honor."

"Well, at least there's one thing we can both agree on, Erin," I spat out.

"Erin, *please*." Maria raised her hands and let them fall to her sides with an exasperated sigh. "Just shut up. We can't stand here arguing all day and you're not going to change her mind any more than she is yours."

"Maybe you should be the one to shut up, Maria," Erin snapped.

The women glared at each other, animosity that probably went back more years than I'd been alive, simmering between them. If looks could kill, Maria and Erin would have dropped dead in the middle of the aisle as they glared daggers at one another.

Galen laughed, seemingly enjoying the show as he licked bacon grease from his fingers.

"Are you going to come with us, or do we need to have one of the guards brought in?" Erin said finally as rested her hands on her rounded hips with a dramatic huff.

"That depends on where we're going," I answered, leaning against Galen's cage and crossing my arms over my still-naked chest.

"Bjorn has arranged for you to meet the princesses from the other packs. They're participating in your coronation and wedding ceremonies," Maria explained in an awed and cheerful tone, as if I should have been excited about the upcoming festivities.

"Then the answer is no," I told them before bending down in front of the barred window of Galen's crate to speak directly to him. "Whatever happens, I want you to know that I love you."

"I love you too, baby."

Bolstered by the declaration of his feelings for me in front of two members of the Bone Pack, I steeled my spine, went back to my cage and crawled inside.

"I knew she'd be like this. Just like her mother." Erin grumbled her complaints to Maria, the only person in the room remotely willing to listen.

"Flattery will get you nowhere, Erin." I chuckled and took advantage of the added legroom while the crate door was open, and scooted against the back wall, stretching my legs out in front of me with a sigh.

"Maybe you should go, Talia." Galen said, speaking quickly before I could shoot down his suggestion. "It can't hurt to meet some of the pack members. We still need information."

"Do you see, Maria?" Erin huffed. "I mean, are you listening to this? She's openly agreeing to be a spy for the Long Claw pack! We need to tell Bjorn about this immediately."

"Erin," said Maria grinding out her colleague's name. "Are you familiar with the old adage, you catch more flies with honey than—"

"If you're asking me to be nice to this woman after everything she's said and done in the short time she's been here, my answer is going to be a resounding 'no'." Erin pulled a gray knit Bernie hat out of her coat pocket and jammed it over her curly auburn hair.

"The feeling is mutual, bitch." I crawled back out of my cage and rifled through the arctic gear they'd brought along for me. I decided to take Galen's advice and go with the women from the Bone Pack in the hopes of unraveling the secrets of the Deofol pack and their role in the demon wolf god's plan.

And with any luck I might make some allies to aid us in our escape.

It was crystal clear Erin would not be fulfilling that role. She'd made her allegiances plain as day and was definitely on Team Bjorn. The jury was still out on Maria. Out of the two of them, she seemed more concerned with winning over her pack's heir and that gave me something to work with.

Perhaps she can be swayed to my cause.

"How many princesses are there?" I asked casually. "Does each of the demon packs have one?" I pinched the hem of the coat they'd provided together and zipped it up over my layers of warm clothing.

"Yes and no," Maria offered before her pack mate could come up with another snarky remark. "Each pack has an heir, but the official title of Princess is reserved for the demon wolf god's chosen bride."

Wonderful.

I stood in the way of the other heirs' ascension to full princess —a status I'd already made clear I wanted no part of.

So much for making friends or allies.

I hated leaving Galen alone in the kennels. It was freezing, filthy, and stank to high heaven. And worst of all it felt like a betrayal, leaving him locked up in such a manner while I roamed free. Or as free as a person could be with two chaper-one-guards in an encampment full of hostiles. But my situation certainly beat the four-by-three metal box I was forced to leave him in.

Maria and Erin escorted me across the encampment from the kennels to a large arched building with an architectural style that mimicked an igloo.

"This is our meeting hall." Maria opened the airlock and stepped inside the tunnel. "This is where we hold all of our community gatherings and ceremonies. It's considered neutral ground."

"Are there problems among the factions?" I asked, staying close to Maria, preferring her company to Erin's.

The latter shadowed me and pulled up the rear.

"No more than your average pack." Maria shed several layers

until she was down to a pair of black, wool dress slacks and a black scoop-neck cashmere sweater.

Their pack is far from average—just like our problems.

"You have territory disputes here?" I asked, unable to hide my surprise that anyone would fight over what amounted to a massive ice-skating rink with outbuildings. I missed the grass that covered the fields and the woodlands that surrounded the Long Claw's territory. I missed the sound of rural nightlife, like owls and crickets and even the bullfrogs croaking out their evening chorus.

The Deofol territory was ice and snow in every direction. A literal frozen wasteland of doom. The only sounds to break the eerie quiet of their arctic environment were the generators and the sled dogs. I hadn't even spotted any bird life, no kites or artic eagles. As far as I was concerned there was nothing to fight over.

This place is an icy shit hole.

"Our territory is rich with resources. Do you know how much revenue Prudhoe Bay generates from the oil fields? The Deofol pack controls *all* of that. We run the drilling operations, the refineries. All of it. There are millions of reasons why the packs fight and they all involve barrels or dollar bills." Maria opened the interior door leading to a sprawling antechamber.

Basket lights were suspended from the ceiling by long steel cables and cast a soft, natural glow throughout the open space. Lush fabrics and furs decorated their meeting room. It was a welcome contrast to the harsh, unforgiving outdoors, and grotesque and unkempt kennels.

"Don't look so shocked, Princess Talia." Erin spat out my title like it left a bitter taste in her mouth and rolled her eyes. "We have heat and running water too. We're not living in the dark ages."

"Your Alpha is trying to force me to marry a demon god. That's pretty dark, Erin," I fired back, engaging the same tone and emphasis on her name that she'd graced mine with.

"We brought you to the meeting house as the Alpha asked. We fulfilled our duty to the Bone Pack. You're on your own, now." Erin grabbed Maria by the arm and pulled her to the side. "Come on, leave her. I need a drink."

Maria looked as though she wanted to apologize for her pack-mate's behavior, but Erin whisked her away before she had the chance.

An awkward hush fell over the room, conversations coming to an abrupt halt, as everyone in the packed room turned their attention to me. The crowd parted into three distinct groups that I assumed represented the three different packs. Everyone in attendance was dressed in their ceremonial best. Except for me.

My fleece lined jeans and plaid flannel shirt were a far cry from the suits and sweater dresses worn by the rest of the event's attendees. Which I suspected was not an accident. I searched the sea of faces for Erin's and found her smirking at me over the rim of a clear plastic cup.

"Bitch." I mouthed the word, hoping she could read my lips.

Erin raised her cup in mock salute and downed its contents.

"Welcome, Princess Talia, daughter of the Bone Pack and heir to the throne." Bjorn's baritone voice boomed through the room and commanded the full attention of every wolf in his pack. "This is a joyous occasion. After too many years without a true heir, the Bone Pack can finally fulfill their obligation and satisfy our god."

The group of wolves in the center of the room dipped their heads and bowed to their Alpha, only for a familiar face to rise and address her leader.

Valerie.

"It is not an obligation but an honor, Alpha. The Bone Pack offers our heir willingly." The silver haired beauty I'd met weeks before dropped into a deep and flawless curtsey, sparing a sideways glance in my direction. She'd never mentioned anything about the Bone Pack or her allegiance to it when she approached me at the summit.

The nefarious plan she'd concocted with her brother Victor back in Montana suddenly became crystal clear. They had planted the seed of curiosity and teased me with just enough information to lure me here with the intention of offering me up to their demon wolf god once I showed up.

I felt like a first-rate sucker and worse for having drawn Galen into this with me.

"We thank you for your family's loyalty," said Bjorn wrapping up his welcome speech, before encouraging everyone to enjoy themselves and the festivities.

"Talia, it's wonderful to see you again," cooed Valerie as she moved with a fluid grace, gliding across the floor to approach me. "Victor was sure we'd over played our hand and you wouldn't come... but here you are."

"Oh, you played your part quite well, Valerie," I ground out between clenched teeth and a forced smile. "My aunt warned me not to come, but I followed your little trail of breadcrumbs like a fool."

"Sylvia?" Valerie slipped her arm through mine and clasped her hands together. "I haven't spoken to her in ages. I think I heard she settled somewhere in Nebraska or maybe it was Iowa. How's she doing?"

"She's fine," I responded with a clipped tone. There was no way I was dishing the gossip or giving her the scoop on my aunt. What loyal family I had left; I would protect to my last breath.

I suspected Valerie was simply digging for information and I wasn't going to hand it over willingly. The Deofol pack didn't take kindly to deserters and the Bone Pack had lost two important wolves when my mother and her sister ran away. They eventually caught up with my mother, but my aunt had managed to give them the slip all these years.

And good on her.

Sylvia had stayed off their radar successfully my whole life, and I had no intention of being the one who gave her up. She had told Galen and I not to come. She'd warned us that the demon wolf packs lived up to their names.

We should have listened.

"Let me introduce you to the other princesses. They're just dying to meet you." Valerie started toward the pack clustered together on our left. "The Blood Pack," she introduced.

"I thought they were called heirs and not princesses?" I let my arm go limp and slid it through the crook of her elbow, refusing to take even one step toward the other pack members.

"They are, but in your absence, both were presented to the demon wolf God and assumed the title. But you bear his marks and by rights the title is officially yours." She glanced at my arm and then at my feet which were unmoving and firmly planted on the floor. "Come now, don't be a child, Talia." She slid her hand down my arm and encircled my wrist. "The only person you're making this hard for is yourself."

Her red painted nails pierced the skin on the inside of my wrist as she tightened her grip and pulled me toward the Blood Pack. "Princess Andrea, this is Princess Talia. Princess Talia, this is Andrea." Valerie made a sweeping gesture with her hand to acknowledge the rest of the group. "And this is the Blood Pack, obviously." She seemed far more interested in parading me around like a trophy than making genuine introductions.

"The lost heiress returns. So nice of you to grace us with your presence after all these years." Andrea's fiery hair matched the flames of rage burning in her eyes. "What a coincidence, Valerie running into you at the national summit like that."

Andrea's tone implied that she believed my chance encounter with the silver-haired siblings was anything but. I'd begun to suspect the same thing myself, but I'd be damned if I gave her the satisfaction of saying so.

"Imagine my surprise to find another demon wolf in attendance," said Valerie, swooping in and seizing control of the conversation. "She looks so much like her mother, doesn't she? There was just *no* mistaking who she was when I laid on her. I knew she was our missing heir. And to learn that she'd been marked... the first *true* princess in years!"

"How fortunate for the Bone Pack. Now, If you'll excuse me, Bjorn is free and I haven't greeted our Alpha properly." Andrea pushed between us, knocking me with her shoulder on her way past.

"Come along, Talia." Valerie ignored the intentional slight, along with the rest of the Blood Pack's members and steered me toward the next group of people.

"Speaking of the summit, I don't recall seeing Bjorn there," I said. I had my suspicions about Valerie's plan, but there were still pieces missing from the puzzle and I needed her to clear them up. The more information we had to work with, the better.

"We don't belong to the alliance. Victor and I were asked to attend and speak as experts in the field of demons," she explained with a casual smile as if treason were an everyday occurrence.

"I'm sure the information you provided was invaluable," I quipped, sarcasm dripping from my every word.

"Spoken like a true royal. You're a natural at this." Valerie pointed out the heiress for the third pack. "The raven-haired beauty is Jacinda," she offered. "The Fang Pack have been business partners and political allies with our pack for centuries."

Despite their alliances, my reception with the Fang Pack went about as well as it had with the Blood Pack. I was neither welcomed nor wanted by any of the other demon wolf pack members. I'd hoped to make alliances of my own, but the only remotely friendly face in the crowd was Valerie's—and that friendliness was as obviously fake as the day was long.

It seemed Galen and I were on our own. Somehow, we needed to come up with a plan to escape, preferably before Galen had to fight Bjorn in the challenge... and before I was mated to the demon wolf god.

CHAPTER 14

GALEN

Talia had been gone for hours and I was out of my mind with worry.

My wolf stirred, treading on my already frayed nerves as he paced the dark corners of my mind.

I would have done the same had I not been confined to this tiny metal box. The longer we stayed with the Deofol pack, the weaker my bond with Talia seemed to be. I reached out several times, but I couldn't hear her thoughts or feel her emotions. I could however sense her presence at the other end of the tattered thread that connected us. She was still alive. That would have to be enough to satisfy us until she was with us again.

My ears perked at the sound of the main door opening, but I was met with disappointment when I caught the scent of another guard and not my mate. That made two shift changes since she'd left which was strange.

The new guard made the rounds, dishing out bowls of salmon and root vegetable scraps for me and the sled dogs confined in the cages around me. It was the best meal I'd had since we surrendered ourselves to the Deofol pack, outside of the half-plate of breakfast Talia had saved for me.

Grateful for the small and simple comfort of having a full stomach and enough protein to refuel my body, I forced my eyes closed and willed myself to sleep. The relief of rest didn't come easy or last for very long. Even in sleep my mind still managed to play out every possible scenario of why Talia had been gone so long and what could have happened to her.

The familiar *whoosh* and *click* of the airlock opening and closing echoed through the building, but I refused to get my hopes up—until the faint smell of honeysuckle permeated the air.

Talia!

She'd been brought back under the escort of two wolves I recognized from the summit—Victor and Valerie—the same wolves who had set Talia and I on the path to finding the demon wolf pack in the first place.

Seeing them flanking Talia, it was obvious now what had happened. They had purposely sought her out at the summit and fed her just enough information to make sure she found her way here to the pack; but not enough to give her any hint of the danger she'd face if and when she returned to this pack.

"Galen!" As soon as she saw me, she broke free of their grip, rushed to my cage and reached through the bars without hesitation. Her soft fingertips grazed my cheek before finding my lips. "Have they let you out at all?" she asked, her brows furrowed with concern.

"For a few minutes. Just enough to stretch my legs," I lied, knowing full well she would sniff out the truth eventually, but the truth seemed pointless when it would only serve to upset her.

"Let him out," she demanded as she pushed herself to her feet, rounding on her escorts with her finger pointed. "I know you two know the code. Open the cage. *Now.*"

"I think her new title has gone to her head," Victor chuckled, flicking his gaze from Talia to his sister and back again. "We're about to lock you back in your cage, Princess. You're not really in a position to go ordering us around."

"Oh, just open the door and let him out," said Valerie as she let out an exasperated sigh. She walked to the back wall and retrieved one of the cattle prods. "If we grant you this small favor, Talia, we expect you to do us one in return."

"What kind of favor?" she countered. Much to my relief, Talia appeared to be thinking with her head and not just her heart and asked for terms before she agreed to anything. If she wanted to survive, there needed to be a limit to what my freedom—especially a temporary one—would cost her.

"I reserve the right to call the marker in at a time of my choosing." Valerie tapped the end of the cattle prod against her palm. "That's my only offer and it's non-negotiable."

I watched as the hope drained from her eyes. I was helpless inside my cage to do anything to console her, except for to refuse before she could make a mistake and accept the offer. "No," I said, raising my voice. My muscles cramped in protest at the lost opportunity, but I refused to have Talia indebted to either of them because of me.

"Galen, let me—"

"I'm fine." I lied again, disappointed with how easy it was to do now that our bond was left hanging in tatters. But her happiness and safety were on the line and I needed to step up in the only way I could. She deserved nothing less than my complete honesty and I had failed her. Just like I'd failed to protect her from Bjorn and the demon wolf god.

"See, princess, he's fine." Victor strolled over to her cage and unlocked the door. "If you would be so kind?"

Talia knelt before my cage, pressed her face against the bars and kissed every inch of my skin available to her through the narrow gaps.

Victor cleared his throat and coughed into his fisted hand. "Princess."

She left my cage for her own on the opposite side of the aisle without fuss and crawled inside.

Victor entered the code, took the cattle prod from his sister and returned it to its place hanging from a hook on the wall before escorting Valerie out, leaving us alone.

"You've been locked up in there this whole time, haven't you?" Talia asked as she peered through the bars of her cage, daring me to lie to her face again.

"Yes." I sighed, unable to hold her gaze or tell another lie, and pressed my forehead against the cold metal door of my crate. "But they're going to have to let me out of here eventually to use the bathroom or clean up the mess if they don't."

"Galen, you should have at least let me try to set you free. Just because Valerie said the offer was non-negotiable, doesn't mean it actually was." She turned to her side and mirrored my position. Strands of her golden-red hair spilling out of the spaces between the bars in the window.

"Tell me about the gathering. Gain any intel or find any prospective allies?" I asked, avoiding the argument I knew was coming and changed the subject.

"No to finding any allies." She sighed and let her head fall back. "I'm pretty sure everyone here hates me. Well, almost everyone. Valerie and Victor seem like they have taken an interest in me for their own reasons."

"Exactly. It's because they have an ulterior motive." I wasn't telling her anything she didn't already know. Talia was a smart woman and would have already figured that out on her own. "And I find it hard to believe everyone hates you. It's impossible to hate you."

"Well, apparently, now that I've returned, the other princesses have had their titles revoked. They're back to being regular heirs to their respective clan packs, because that title is reserved for the chosen one. Lucky me."

I didn't need to see her clearly to know that she'd rolled her eyes when she said that. "Okay, so maybe the other princesses— former princesses—hate you," I teased, finding it easier to laugh —and breathe—since Talia had returned unharmed. "How about information? Any loose lips at the soirée? Hopefully, Boot Hill isn't a dry town. Alcohol works like a truth serum and gets people talking."

"I don't think there's enough alcohol in the whole of Alaska to make anyone in the Deofol pack talk to me. I'm not even joking. They hate me, take my word for it." She sighed. "I probably shouldn't say this, but I'm glad they don't like me. I don't want to belong here."

"Good, because you *don't* belong here." It pained me not to be able to pull her close and wrap my arms around her. "You belong to me and the Long Claw pack. We chose you and love you. *I* love you, Talia Linetti and that's never going to change."

"I love you too." She pressed her fingers to her lips and proceeded to blow me a kiss. "I did find out one interesting tidbit of information, but I think it qualifies more as gossip than actual news."

"Sometimes gossip turns out to be actual news. Hit me with it and we'll see if it's noteworthy." I rubbed my calf, working out the knot in the cramped muscle, and listened with earnest. I hoped it was news we could use and that we had finally caught a break.

"The Deofol pack isn't a member of the alliance which is why we never crossed paths with Bjorn in Montana. Victor and Valerie were invited to the summit by the council as experts on demons and to help educate other packs."

"Huh, I don't recall seeing their names listed on the itinerary or hearing them speak at any of the meetings I attended." I raked my fingers through my hair, scratching at my scalp as I worked through a thought nagging at my brain. "Did you see them anywhere outside of the social events or when they approached you specifically?"

"Umm, I don't know. I mean, I spent most of the trip at the cabin or attending the networking events with you. I probably wouldn't have crossed paths with them if they hadn't sought me out, but we know why they did that now. Why do you ask? What are you thinking?"

I could almost hear Talia's brain working through the bond. I hated not knowing exactly what she was thinking and missed the depth of the connection we'd shared. She was there, in my mind, but *just* agonizingly out of reach. It was as infuriating and frustrating as it was heartbreaking.

"Do you think it really was just a coincidence, them running into you at a summit about demons attacking the packs?" I scrubbed my face with my hands, the stubble along my cheeks and jaw scratching my palms. "Or something more?"

"You don't believe in coincidences." Talia found the end of the frayed thread between us and held on tight. She poured more of herself into the connection, strengthening our bond as much as possible without physical contact. "You think they planned the whole thing? That they went to the summit to find me specifically? But how would they have known I would be there?"

"I think the first demon that marked you was sent by their demon wolf god, and the mark works like some sort of beacon." It all seemed far-fetched even for our witch an shifter filled world, but I couldn't come up with a more logical or fitting explanation.

"The demon equivalent of being chipped." Talia barked out a bitter laugh. "Demon marks, beacons, demon wolf packs and sacrifices to gods. How insane is this? If we weren't here right now... I mean, if someone else tried to tell me that this happened to them, I'd probably say they were nuts."

"I know. The whole thing sounds crazy, but I can't come up with another explanation for how Victor and Valerie ended up at the summit. The council wouldn't have called on a non-member pack to offer expert advice." I stifled a groan and shifted my weight to one side, trying to stretch out again. The muscle aches and pains were becoming more than a nuisance; they were so painful that they were affecting my train of thought. I needed to keep a clear head if we were going to make it out of Boot Hill unscathed.

"We have to get out of here, Galen." Talia echoed my thoughts and gripped the bars of her crate. "What about Marcus? Can you reach him through the pack bonds? He'll rally the pack and come looking for us! I'm sure of it."

"I didn't want to worry you, but..." I struggled to find the right words and regretted not telling her after we'd promised to be honest with each other after she told me the truth about her wolf's red eyes. But I hadn't been able to bring myself to rip the single shred of hope from her. Not when I wasn't entirely certain myself that the pack bond was truly broken.

"I've already tried but it's like the line is disconnected. Something or someone is blocking me from reaching the other members of the pack. This is the farthest I've ever been from the pack. Maybe the distance is too great? I don't know."

"What if they did something to you to foil the bond? Maybe they're putting something in your food?" Talia offered, continuing to surprise me with her grit and determination. Rather than give up, she came up with a possible solution. "I think you should skip breakfast. I know it'll be hard, but see if you feel any different and then try calling out through the bond again."

"I haven't felt sick or drowsy after eating. So, I don't think it's the food, but at this point I'm willing to try anything." I didn't want to shoot down her idea, but we couldn't put all our hopes for escaping the Deofol pack in my Alpha bond. "But Talia, I can only skip so many meals before I become useless to both of us. We're going to need a back-up plan."

Talia fell silent for a time, the quiet stretching between us before she spoke again. "What if I accept my title and become the Bone Pack Princess for real?" Talia's voice wavered, as if she was uncertain about the plan she was forming and rightly so. "That has to come with certain power privileges, right?"

"I don't think the privilege that comes with that role is for you," I growled, anger burning in my gut at the thought of the demon wolf god laying as much as a finger on my mate.

"We have to try, Galen. If we don't, you'll die in that cage, and I'll be forced into marriage with the demon wolf god." Talia turned her head to the side and pressed her ear against the window of her crate. "Someone's coming," she breathed.

"It's now or never," I answered keeping my voice low. "We make our move, find an opportunity. No matter who comes through that door." Being the expendable party in this artic equation, I knew the stakes better than anyone. Talia was right. We had to try something. We couldn't wait for a rescue team that wasn't even coming or hold onto hope that someone in the Deofol pack would see reason.

We have to save ourselves.

The door to the kennel opened and two guards entered, armed with tranquilizer guns and hunting knives.

"Time to hit the latrine. You know the drill." One of the guards stepped in front of my cage, tapping the tranquilizer gun holstered on his waist. "Be a good dog and don't give us any trouble. I'd hate to kill you in front of the princess."

I waited for him to unlock the door, biding my time and followed commands until an opportunity presented itself.

The second guard stepped in front of Talia's cage, blocking her from my view.

Two against one.

Ordinarily, I'd like those odds, but they were both armed and that tipped the balance in their favor. Not to mention I was in a ton of pain, having been cramped up like a mutt for so long. A fight wouldn't be easy... Still, it was the best chance I had to get Talia and myself out of the kennels and I knew I had to take it. I crawled out of my cage, pushing through the pain of cramped and stiff muscles, and got slowly to my feet.

"Good boy." The guard pulled the tranquilizer gun from his hip holster, aimed and shoved me forward with his free hand toward the bathroom at the front of the kennel building.

The other guard removed his gloves and knelt in front of Talia's cage, reaching for a strand of her hair that draped through the bars of her window. "I can see why our god chose you." The golden-red lock of her hair slipped through his fingers. "So beautiful. If you weren't spoken for, I'd sure as hell like a taste."

"What the hell are you doing, Eric?" The first guard risked a glance over his shoulder at his partner. "Get the fuck away from her cage."

That is it.

My one chance, and my wolf was as ready as I was to take it. He answered my call and burst free of my human form. The transformation was mortally excruciating, but came faster than any shift I'd ever experienced before. Together, we pushed through the pain and lunged into action, seizing the small window of opportunity the second guard's distraction had provided.

Without hesitation I gave myself over to my wolf and let his instincts take over. In an instant we were off the floor and lunging for the guard's neck.

He fired the tranq gun, but it was too late. The dart skidded across the floor uselessly, missing its mark by a wide berth.

My wolf did not. Blood filled my mouth, the copper tang coating my tongue, as my teeth sank into his neck. My jaws clamped shut, head shaking back and forth as I ripped a large chunk of flesh free. Bite after vicious bite, I tore into his neck until his jugular was severed and he collapsed beneath me in a pool of blood.

The snow dogs barked and howled, egging me on like the crowd at a prize boxing match.

"What the fu—" The second guard's shout was cut short.

I pounced, a flash of fang and fur, and took him to the ground. Biting down, my teeth found purchase in the soft muscle of his cheek. A unexpected pain blossomed in my side.

The guard had drawn his knife before we hit the floor and buried it to the hilt just below my ribs. He pulled up and out, the serrated edge scraping against the underside of my rib. He raised up again in desperation, driving the knife in again and pulled the blade, creating a grizzly, long gash along my side.

Blood seeped from my wounds, matting my fur and coating the floor as he grappled for control of the fight. I used everything at my disposal, fangs and claws, but I was losing blood faster than I could heal. I was in very real danger of bleeding out and my opponent sensed it. So did my mate.

Talia cried for mercy, begging the guard to stop as she shook the bars of her crate.

Her sobs and pleas for him not to kill me, spurred me on, giving me and my wolf the push we needed to finish him. I *would* die for her—but not before I set her free. With a renewed surge of self-worth and determination my teeth and nails tore into his flesh without remorse. I held nothing back, I let my beast reign until the fight left the guard's body and his face was unrecognizable.

I collapsed on top of him, my body heaving, tongue lolling to one side of my mouth as I panted. Black spots danced along my vision. Exhaustion and blood loss threatened to pull me under, but I forced my eyes open and crawled on my belly to Talia's cage. Despite the damage done, my body began to heal itself. Muscles and skin knit together, and the bleeding stopped sooner than I'd expected. But I was in no condition to shift back and I couldn't manipulate the lock on her cage in my wolf form.

She's still trapped. I've failed her yet again.

I needed more time, but time was something we didn't have.

The door opened and three more guards rushed in.

One of them opened fire and hit me with a tranquilizer dart in my hind leg, finding it's mark nice and easy as I lay prone and exhausted.

The other two guards grabbed me by the scruff of my neck and dragged me away from Talia's cage.

The one that had shot me advanced past us, unlocked Talia's crate, grabbed her by the ankle and yanked her out.

Her screams as she was being hauled bodily away was the last sound I heard before my world went black and I lost consciousness.

CHAPTER 15
TALIA

My head spun like a top And I pressed my palms against my temples to slow the pounding drums inside my skull. I nestled into the soft down pillows and duvet, pulling the covers over my eyes to block the assaulting light blaring in through the large window with its curtains drawn all the way over to the opposite sides of the room.

Wait... what? Pillows? Blankets?

Neither comfort had been afforded to Galen or I since we'd arrived here. The vicious headache rolling through my mind like a runaway freight train made it difficult to concentrate, but I clawed my way through, processing my situation as best I could.

I battled the nausea roiling in my stomach and sat up, taking in my surroundings slowly as clarity returned at a snail's pace. I'd been moved from the kennels and into a posh bedroom with no recollection of the transition happening. The cotton mouth and unquenchable thirst, combined with my other symptoms confirmed my suspicions that I'd been drugged. They'd obviously sedated me after Galen...

The last thing I remembered was watching Galen fight for his life, and my freedom, against two guards in the kennels. He'd been stabbed—almost gutted—and had lost so much blood.

Too much blood.

He'd crawled to me, a broken man, and collapsed in front of my cage. His coat was matted with red, his eyes half-lidded and his breathing shallow. Fear and pain unlike I'd ever experienced gripped my heart with a cruel vice-like grip. They'd killed him! My mate, the man, and the wolf to whom I'd pledged my life was gone... he could not have survived, I was sure of it. He' been lying in a crimson pool of his own spent life. The memory almost made me sick.

I ripped back the covers and tumbled out of the four-poster bed, collapsing under my own body weight. The drugs were clearly still in my system and if I was going to survive, I needed to shift to burn the sedatives from my system. In desperation I called to my wolf, begging her to come forth and heal us of the sickening, drug-fucked sensation that had me feeling like I was clawing my way through a whirlpool of sludge. But she didn't answer.

The magic inherent in all wolves that binds our animal and human forms was still there. My wolf was definitely still there. I felt her presence in my mind, but no matter how many times I tried, she refused to answer my call. Whatever drugs the guards had given me, did more than just knock me out. They'd incapacitated my wolf, all but tranquilizing her. I'd essentially been stripped of my ability to heal and defend myself.

Fuck!

The Deofol pack had taken my wolf *and* my mate from me. They'd taken everything and left me broken and at their mercy. And the mercy of their demon wolf god.

"Oh, good. You're awake." Valerie strolled into the room with an arm full of towels and what appeared to be beauty products. "We need to get you ready for your big day and, I hate to say it, but we do have our work cut out for us."

"Where is my mate?" I managed. I needed to see his body, to see for myself that he was truly gone. I craved that closure more than air. He was yet one more loved one with no place to mark their life and death except the scar their passing had left on my heart.

Valerie tittered. "He's waiting for you, Talia." She set the stack of towels on a chaise lounge and piled the products beside them. "Which is why we need to get you prepared for the blessing ritual and then the mating ceremony."

For a moment I thought she was talking about Galen and my heart leapt, only to shatter all over again when I realized she was talking about her damned god. "I won't marry him. I won't." I pushed myself to my feet and stood my ground as best as I could on my two wobbly legs. "You can force me to stand at an altar, but I will never say the words. I'll never bind myself to him! I'll cut out my tongue first."

"Oh please, don't be so dramatic, Princess." Valerie disappeared behind a door on the opposite side of the room and returned a moment later, the sound of rushing water following her. "I'm drawing you a bath. A nice long soak will do you a world of good."

"You're delusional!" I raged with what little strength I had left and rushed to the door, rattling the doorknob and pounding my fist against the wooden panels. "I will never stop trying to escape. Never! Do you hear me?" The loss of Galen and my wolf was too much bear on top of everything else... my father, Max, my mother, countless loyal pack members...

"It's *just* a bubble bath, Talia. There's no one waiting in the bathroom to perform a surprise wedding ceremony, I promise you." Valerie sighed and collected the bottles of shampoo and conditioner. "I understand how overwhelmed you are with your new role and responsibility. If I could switch places with you I would, gladly, but the demon wolf god did not choose me."

"I'd already chosen my mate, Valerie." I clutched the door-knob, holding on for dear life, as my world dropped out from under me. "My heart, my soul, it will always belong to Galen."

"A queen is allowed her consorts, Talia. So, think on that before you throw your life away. As a consort you have no rights, no power, but all that changes when you wear the crown." She turned on her heel and walked into the bathroom, disappearing from sight once more.

"I don't want consorts!" I marched after her, furious that she would suggest I take another wolf as a lover, as if that might comfort me. "I wanted no one but Galen, and you've taken him from me—just like you've taken everything else!"

"We merely separated the two of you after your last escape attempt. Surely, even you can understand that precaution? You act as though we killed him in cold blood, child." She ran her hand through the cloud of bubbles floating on the surface of the bath water, before glancing over her shoulder. "Wait, you thought he was dead?"

He's not dead?

My heart leapt at the shock of that news. "Of course, I thought he was dead! I can't feel him through our pack bond anymore." Was she really telling the truth about Galen or was this yet another ploy to garner my compliance? "The last time I saw him he was lying in a pool of his own blood."

"I can't speak for the Alpha's plans for him," Valerie admitted. "But as of this moment in time Galen is still alive."

My heart raced at the realization that he wasn't dead, but after everything Valerie had done, it wasn't like I couldn't fully trust this woman either. "Take me to him." I wanted—no, *needed* —proof of life and the only proof I would accept was seeing him with my own two eyes.

"And if I do that, if I take you to him, what are you willing to do for me?" She flicked the water in the tub pointedly, splashing it onto the marble tile tub surrounds.

With a deep breath, I set my jaw, stripped out of my clothes, stepped over the side of the soaker tub and sank into the steamy water.

I'll play along for as long as it benefits me.

"There's a good girl," she crooned. "Now, lean your head back." Valerie raised a white porcelain pitcher and poured hot water over my head, soaking my hair. "What do you know about our god?" she asked.

"Nothing." It didn't cost me anything to admit I was entirely ignorant of their ways. My mother had gone rogue and run away from the Deofol pack. That told me all that I needed to know as far as I was concerned. This pack was obviously one to be feared.

You're all fucking insane.

"He is a benevolent god, Talia. Believe me when I say he will treat you like the goddess that you are." Valerie squeezed a puddle of shampoo, that smelled of rosehip and bergamot, into her hand and lathered it into my long golden-red hair.

"He's cursed witches, attacked innocent people, *and* wolves. Do you call that benevolent?" I asked. "I think we might have very different definitions of what that word means." I swiped the back of my hand against my forehead to stop a trail of bubbles from reaching my eyes.

"No wonder you're so resistant to marriage! That couldn't be further from the truth." Valerie refilled the pitcher from the faucet and rinsed the shampoo from my hair. "Our god isn't the one responsible for the curses or the attacks. His *wife* is," she explained as if that truth was the most obvious fact in the world.

"I'm sorry, what? His *wife*?" I rounded on her in the tub, sending a wave of bathwater splashing over the side. "He's already mated? Then why would he take another?"

"He's a god, Talia. It's not our place to question why." Valerie took me by the shoulders, easing me around until she had access to my hair again and applied a generous amount of conditioner. "The goddess is a cruel and jealous creature by nature. She fell out of favor with our god but refuses to let go of her position and power. If you are looking for someone to blame, it should be her, not your future husband."

My mind reeled, struggling to process what Valerie had just revealed. First and foremost, Galen was alive. Secondly, the demon wolf god was not responsible for the curses and demon attacks... and thirdly, it was the demon god's wife all along. He had a wife.

A demon wolf goddess.

Stories of Zeus and Hera came to mind, the classic tale of a woman scorned. I scoured my brain for anything else in the myth that could help me, but I couldn't recall a single tale where Hera had shown mercy to Zeus's mortal lovers or given them their freedom back. She'd cursed them all and made them suffer, as if it were *their* fault the King of the Gods, himself, had pursued them.

Something told me it would be the exact same story with the Deofol pack's goddess. Blinded by the love of her mate and burning with jealousy over his desire to claim a mortal bride, she'd taken out her rage in the only way she could—on the mortals. Our packs, our allies, and the towns we called home, bore the brunt of her rage over her mate's indiscretions.

But if he was already mated, then the blame lay equally and as squarely on the demon god's shoulders as it did hers. Valerie had made the demon wolf goddess out to be the villain of her story, but I found myself already disagreeing. The blame for the death and destruction happening should be laid at the god's feet as much as his wife's.

Though, Valerie was right about one thing. The bath had done wonders for me. It had given me an opportunity to glean information I might not have otherwise and afforded me the opportunity to clear my head.

And while Valerie ran a comb through my freshly conditioned hair, an idea began to form. It was crazy and likely to get me killed, but if Galen and I were going to have a future together, it was something I had to try. I just needed a little more time—something Galen and I never seemed to have enough of. But I was finally starting to put the pieces of the puzzle together and if I played my cards right, the attacks would stop, and my mate and I would be able to walk out of Boot Hill together.

"Thank you, Valerie," I said. "You were right, I do feel better." My gratitude was genuine, but not in the way she expected. Valerie had hoped to convince me that I was chosen for a great honor. And in a way, I supposed she was right. I had been chosen —to bring an end to the Deofol pack and their gods.

"You're welcome, Princess. It's an honor to attend to your needs before the ceremony." She grabbed one of the large, plush towels and held it open, turning her head to the side to offer me a modicum of privacy.

"When can I see Galen?" I stepped out of the tub and into the towel, wrapping it around my body.

"I doubt we'll have time before the blessing ritual." Valerie motioned to a small wooden stool and reached for a paddle brush on the vanity to shine up my hair.

"You promised," I accused, grabbing her wrist and jerking her forward. The brush fell from her hands and clattered against the tiled floor. "And you are going to keep that promise, aren't you?" I caught a glimpse of my red-eyed reflection in the mirror, but for once I didn't shirk away from the woman staring back at me. The Deofol wolf on my mother's side was as much a part of me as the rogue wolf on my father's side. It was time I accepted her. Besides, I had more than enough actual demons to fight. I sure as hell didn't need to add personal ones to the battle.

"Talia. Calm down." Valerie's confidence wavered, along with the strength in her voice. Her fingers trembled as she grasped my arm in return. "I only said we wouldn't have time *before* the blessing. I never said I wouldn't take you. I know I haven't given you much reason to trust me, but I am a woman of my word. When I give it, I keep it."

I sighed. "Then tell me about the blessing ceremony. What do I have to do?" I released her wrist and adjusted my towel before it slid to the floor.

"You don't have to do anything, really. You simply recite a few words and light some incense. But mostly our priestess will pray over you and offer a blessing on your union to the demon wolf god." Valerie followed me out of the bathroom and retrieved a billowing white gown and matching fur cloak.

The dress had an empire waist heavily embroidered with gold thread in a herringbone-ladder stitch pattern. The long sleeves were slit down the middle from shoulder to wrist and featured similar stitching around the cuffs. "It's beautiful," I breathed in genuine admiration. And it was, but it looked more appropriate for a full-blown wedding ceremony rather than the simple prayer circle Valerie described. "That looks an awful lot like something a bride might wear on her wedding day."

"This?" Valerie held up the dress and spun the hangar in her hand to show off the front and back of the gown. "Your wedding gown is made of the finest silks and Chantilly lace. The essential oils used in the blessing ceremony would ruin it. The white and gold are of this gown represent purity and royalty, that's all. You are the Princess, after all, Talia. There are no expenses spared."

"Well, it's a little late for at least one of those things, Valerie." I pressed the dripping ends of my hair against the towel still wrapped around my body and squeezed out the excess water. "If your god wants a virgin bride, I guess that leaves me out in the cold. Who's the next candidate? The princess from the Blood

Pack? She seemed like an absolute joy. I'm sure the demon wolf god will love her."

"You bear *both* marks, Talia," said Valerie, unamused. "The only person who does not see this as the honor it is, is you."

"I think there are a lot of people outside of the Prudhoe Bay area who would agree with me. You should probably widen your poll to include more zip codes. You'd get more accurate results."

"Talia, the sooner you get ready, the sooner we'll be at the ceremony and the sooner you'll get to see Galen." Valerie's patience had worn thin and with my eyes having returned to their normal shade of violet-blue, so had my threat of violence.

"Fine." I slipped the dress over my head and swept my hair out of the way for Valerie to fasten the buttons on the back.

She plaited my hair into a loose fishtail braid and wove in fresh sprigs of baby's breath and lavender.

"There, all done," she said proudly as she ran her fingers along the crown of my head and smoothed the flyaway strands of hair. "You look beautiful. Fit for a king or a god."

"The only person whose opinion matters to me is Galen's," I growled, hating the thought of him seeing me glammed up for someone other than him.

Bide your time, Talia.

And I would—for Galen, for me, and for the future of a world unplagued by a squabbling pair of demon wolf gods.

Without further ado, Valerie draped the mink and rabbit fur cloak over my shoulders, tied the leather cording to secure it and escorted me to the blessing ceremony.

THE DEOFOL PACK meeting room had been rearranged to accommodate all of the packs and their members. The furniture was gone, and a small wooden altar draped with white and gold linens and fresh greenery took its place. A long gold runner, lined with pillar candles on wrought-iron floor stands, ran down the center of the room, directing me to my destination.

A priestess with a garish and macabre wolf headdress stood behind the altar, her arms outstretched as she beckoned me forward.

Swallowing my fear and dread, I began my walk toward the inevitable. The cloak dragged the ground, rippling the gleaming runner in my wake as I walked down the aisle toward the altar. Again, I was struck by the similarities to what I thought a wedding ceremony would be. Still, it was nothing like I'd imagined my wedding to Galen would be like one day, and for that I was grateful.

The priestess retrieved a brass triangle from beneath the altar and struck it with a metal tuning rod.

A hush fell over the crowd with the first chime. The ceremony had officially begun.

She opened with a prayer in a language I didn't understand and proceeded to light incense, wafting the scented smoke as she walked several circles around me.

The crowd responded, chanting the closing line of her prayer over and over again until the incense burned away.

My head swam. I felt nauseated and dizzy from watching the priestess circle around me like a shark. The lack of food and water in my belly, not to mention the potent scent of the incense, didn't help my condition either. To my relief, the ceremony was brief and ended with a final prayer to the demon wolf god and more triangle chimes.

Bjorn stepped forward then, thanking the priestess for preparing me, the demon wolf god's new bride, for the long-awaited union.

Servers carrying trays laden with glasses filled with ale moved through the room.

"Princess Talia has been returned to us and our packs are truly united once again!" The Alpha raised his silver goblet in a toast. "Tonight, we celebrate."

The Bone Pack, the Blood Pack, and the Fang Pack rejoiced, raising their glasses and clashing them together. The Deofol pack was finally whole. Music played, alcohol flowed, and the pack members danced to the rhythmic beat of the drums.

"This is all for you." Bjorn spoke over the crowd, spearing me with his gaze.

The swaying mass of people parted for their Alpha.

He came over to stand in front of me. "It has been a long time since we have had a crowned Princess among us. Too long."

"What happened to the last one?" I asked, unsure I even wanted to know the real answer. I'd foolishly assumed there hadn't been any other actual brides apart from the goddess herself.

"The demon wolf goddess killed the last princess to accept her husband's proposal, he said before he tipped his goblet back, emptied it of its ale, and signaled for a refill. "The other women chose to be mere consorts over facing the goddess's wrath."

Did that mean I was about to have to fight the demon wolf goddess for something I didn't even want? "You might have mentioned that." I turned to glare at Valerie.

"Would it have changed anything if I did?" Valerie tipped her glass in my direction before she raised it to her lips and took a sip.

As much as I hated to admit it, she was right. It wouldn't have changed a damn thing. I hadn't accepted either role, Princess or consort yet. I wasn't a *willing* participant in any of their mad plans. All I wanted to do was get through the night and see Galen, as promised.

Unfortunately for me, the Alpha of the Deofol pack had other ideas.

· CHAPTER 16
GALEN

I woke up naked and covered in blood. Most of it was mine. It cracked and flaked off my skin, speckling the bottom of my cage like brick-red confetti. New skin had begun to knit over the previously gaping wound in my side while I slept. Taut and tender scar tissue was the only evidence I'd almost been disemboweled the night before. The internal injuries seemed to have healed themselves, thankfully.

I was as good as new. Almost. The only thing that would have completed my healing process and made me whole as man and wolf, would have been to have Talia at my side. Her absence pushed me to the brink of my sanity. My mating bond with Talia was still damaged, and so was our pack bond.

I couldn't hear her in my head anymore or feel the connection with her in my soul. Bjorn or the demon wolf god had done something to weaken our bonds. They wanted to tear us apart and were doing a damned good job of it.

Without any way to communicate with her, I had no idea if she was all right. Every possible scenario, each worse than the last, continually played out in my mind. I assured myself that with or without the bonds between us I would know if something had happened to her—if she'd departed this plane, surely, I would sense that...

So, I clung to the hope that she was alive, unhurt, and as yet unwed. That hope was all that kept me going. At least it was, right up until Bjorn visited me in the kennels and crushed that hope under the heel of his boot without an ounce of mercy.

"I could kill you right now." The Deofol Alpha squatted in front of my crate and rested his arms on his knees. "It would be so easy," he mused. "No one outside of my pack heard the challenge, and no one outside my pack would know what happened to you. And no one in my pack would talk. They're as loyal as wolves come. Really, I should kill you. I'd be a fool not to."

"You would be a fool if you did, Bjorn." I picked at the crusted blood around my fingernail, refusing to meet his gaze and formally acknowledge his presence. "I may not have the support of a false god, but I do have the support of the alliance and my pack knows where I am."

"They may know you're in Alaska, but not precisely where." Bjorn cracked his knuckles, first on his right hand and then his left. "This is wild country, and a lot could happen to a big city wolf like yourself out here. There are things more dangerous than you or me in the Arctic Circle."

I laughed at him, still refusing to look him in the eyes. Both actions were a sign of disrespect. And both were entirely intentional. I wanted to upset and anger him. He clearly wanted me out of the picture, permanently, so I wanted to push him to play his hand.

The Deofol Alpha didn't strike me as the type of wolf who understood discretion.

No, I know his type.

I'd met Alphas like him at alliance functions; wolves that fed on spectacle and were driven by their own ego. Bjorn would want to make an example of me, to remind his wolves what happened to anyone who dared questioned his authority or stepped out of line. He needed them to witness my judgment and my execution —and I knew he would want that especially for Talia.

"True, but my Betas have my itinerary. They knew Talia and I were flying into Prudhoe Bay, and they knew *why*. It won't take long for them to find you and the rest of your pack. The GPS tracker in our gear will probably have sped things along nicely."

"Tracking device, huh?" Bjorn snapped his fingers and ordered one of his guards hovering by the door to come forward. "Find out who checked their gear when they were brought to camp. I want a full accounting of everything they had on them. If there is a tracking device, I want it found. *Now*."

"Too little too late." I stifled a yawn, feigning boredom with our conversation and rolled to my side; essentially giving him my back. "Talia and I are overdue for the rendezvous point. They're closing in on you, mate."

"Did you pass a lot of cell towers on your way through Dead-horse?" It was Bjorn's turn to laugh, but his amusement was genuine and at my expense. "As for satellites, well, if they're even turned toward Prudhoe, you can bet it's on the oil fields. They don't give a shit about what happens out here unless we mess with the refineries or the icebergs. Ironic, since one destroys the other, but that's the way of bureaucracy, isn't it? Sort of like the alliance. They don't give a shit about you, an active member, any more than they do a disenfranchised Alpha like me."

"I guess we'll find out together, then, won't we?" I replied with far more confidence than I felt. There *was* a tracking device in my pack. I had no way of knowing if they'd brought my backpack here, or if it was still back at the boarding house in Deadhorse. If it was, then Bjorn's story about us disappearing in the Alaskan wild stood a chance of playing out.

They were slim, but then, slim was more than none. Hell, it

was more likely than my chances of getting out of this cage alive as far as I could tell.

"Maybe." Bjorn ran his hand over his beard, smoothing the coarse silver hairs. "Or maybe you'll die in battle after all. You really want to challenge me for Alpha? Prove you're worthy enough to stand in a ring with me."

"I'm an Alpha. That's the only proof you need." It seemed Bjorn had forgotten my status. So, I made a point of reminding him.

"I'm familiar with your pack, Galen, and how you came to be Alpha. You inherited your position; unchallenged by anyone in your community. Your wolves are weak. They gave you control without even questioning your authority... and look at you now. Locked in a cage."

"Then let me out and we'll see how long you last in a fair fight." I adjusted my position, turned to face him and finally met his gaze with the full force of my wolf's eyes.

He took the bait. Bjorn punched the code into the keypad and unlocked the door to my crate. He stood, dusted off his pants and stepped back just enough for me to crawl out into the aisle. The other Alpha pressed the sole of his boot against my back and held me down as he spoke to his men. "Get him cleaned up and bring him to the training facility." Bjorn removed his foot from my spine and walked down the aisle toward the exit. "No excessive force unless absolutely necessary. I want him at his best when he enters the ring."

Bjorn's guards reached under my arms, lifted me off the floor and dragged me off to the showers.

The hot water soothed my aching muscles like magic. So, I stayed under the relieving spray until the water ran cold and the pink tinge turned clear as the last traces of my blood disappeared down the drain. I slipped on the basic gray sweatpants they left for me, pulling the drawstring tight around my waist and stepped into a pair of fur lined boots.

One of the guards finished outfitting me with a black sweat-shirt, heavy coat, and a pair of gloves. "Let's go, Long Claw." He hiked up the hem of his coat, revealing a nine-millimeter handgun holstered to his side. "You know the drill and what kind of ammo we're packing. So, just make this easy on all of us, all right?"

I nodded my agreement and followed them out of the kennels, across the main road of the encampment, and into their training facility. It was a large metal prefab building that I estimated to be around four thousand square feet, and most likely the largest building in the Deofol camp perimeter. There were several pieces of workout equipment pushed against the back wall and portable risers set up around a section of the floor covered with tumbling mats.

The guards shoved me forward, pushing me in the direction of the makeshift fighting ring where their Alpha waited with his arms folded over his chest and a smirk on his face.

A large fluorescent light hung from an exposed metal beam that ran along the ceiling to shine a spotlight over the fighting area. A stool, metal bucket, white terry cloth towels, and a water bottle had been placed at either end of the mats—one for each fighter.

People trickled in and filled the tiered bench seats that surrounded the mats.

I scanned the crowd for Talia, but her face wasn't among those peering down at me from the stands. Part of me hoped she wouldn't come. She'd seen more than enough violence. The other part would have killed for just a glimpse of her magnificent violet-blue eyes and breathtaking red-golden hair.

Bjorn pinched his thumb and forefinger together, stuck them in his mouth and let out an ear-piercing whistle.

His pack fell silent, hanging on their Alpha's every word.

"It's been an exciting day for the Deofol pack." He flicked his gaze to me, his lips curled back in a deviant smile, and I knew the excitement he mentioned had something to do with Talia. "But the festivities are far from over." He raised his arms above his head and the crowd cheered and quieted again when he lowered them back down at his side.

"You all recognize the Long Claw Alpha. He has laid down a challenge for this pack and the demon wolf god's betrothed." Bjorn paused for the boos and jeers from his loyal subjects. "But first he must prove his worth. Who among us is willing to put this wolf to the test?"

"I will." A massive hulk of a man who looked more like a descendent of cave trolls than any shifter I'd ever seen, stood with his hand raised.

"Yosef of the Bone Pack." Bjorn acknowledged the contender in the crowd and welcomed him to the opposite side of the mats from me. "Take your place in the ring."

"The Blood Pack is also willing." A second man, half the size of Yosef but no less formidable based on his muscle mass, stepped down from the risers and stood in line.

"Choose your opponent." Bjorn motioned between the two men. "You must defeat them both in hand-to-hand combat before the Deofol pack will acknowledge your challenge for Alpha."

"Yosef." I jerked my head in the direction of the larger wolf.

The bigger they are, the harder they fall.

Or so I hoped.

"Begin!" Bjorn signaled the start of the fight.

The Bone Pack wolf wasted no time hitting the mat. He charged forward, meaty hands clenched into fists in front of his face and elbows tucked in, in guard position.

We danced around the ring, circling each other as we sought out an opening to land the first strike.

Yosef swung with a looping right that any experienced fighter would have seen coming.

I dipped my head and dodged out of the way.

He stepped in again, keeping me on the defensive and swung again.

I dipped left and avoided another headshot but missed the incoming body blow. His fist found its mark and connected with my side. A handful of my ribs cracked on impact and the freshly healed scar threatened to rip wide open. I tucked my elbow in, held it tight against my ribs and kept my guard up as I backpedaled around the mat.

Yosef charged again—but this time I was ready for him.

I unleashed a short right hand to his solar plexus. The punch would have dropped a lesser man to his knees, but Yosef was unfazed.

He rushed in, wrapped me in a crushing bear hug and pinned my arms to my sides. He rolled his hip and threw me to the floor hard enough that my body bounced off the mat like a child's toy. Yosef pounced on the opportunity, taking the fight to the ground, and used his body weight to keep me there. He assumed full mount, centered his mass on my chest and dropped hammer-fist punches to my face.

Blood gushed from my nose, mouth, and a gash along my brow bone, but I refused to yield. I threw body shot after body shot, lasering in on his lower back below his ribs. My eyes had almost swollen shut, but I kept punching until he'd had his fill.

Yosef howled. The relentless kidney shots finally took their toll. He slid to the side and gave up his full mount position.

I bucked beneath him, knocking him the rest of the way off. We grappled on the floor until I worked my way behind him. Slipped my right arm around his neck and clamped my left hand around my wrist, refusing to let go my choke hold.

The warrior from the Bone Pack thrashed and fought, but

before long he dropped, his weight falling on me as he blacked out and went limp in my arms.

I rolled out from under him and pushed myself to my feet. The room swayed—or maybe it was me. Either way, I was minutes from joining the sleeping giant passed out on the mat.

The Blood Pack wolf jumped in swinging before I'd even had a moment to breathe, eager to prove himself to his pack and his Alpha watching from the ringside. Full of energy and injury free, my second opponent had the upper hand, literally and figuratively. He rocked my world with a right uppercut that smacked my jaw together and chipped three teeth.

Fuck.

I'd underestimated the wolf from the Blood Pack and made a tactical error by fighting Yosef first. My plan had been to take the bigger, stronger fighter out of the equation, but in doing so, I'd taken bigger punches and a hell of a lot of damage.

My second opponent moved with the experience of a trained fighter. He was comfortable in the ring and knew how to use every inch to his advantage. Had there been ropes like a traditional boxing ring, he would have had me against them for sure.

For every punch I landed, he landed two. I struggled against his defenses and when I did manage to work my way inside, I was punished with more body shots. The scar on my side may as well have been a red-and-white-ringed bullseye.

He found a soft spot and targeted it, landing jab after vicious jab without remorse.

When I pulled back out of the danger zone, he clocked me with a left haymaker to the temple. Vivid colors danced before my eyes, my knees buckled, and legs went out from under me.

He dove, seizing upon the opportunity and my apparent weakness.

At the last second, I rolled to my side and scrambled to my feet before he could pin me to the floor. The fight felt like it went on for hours. I was exhausted, but somehow began to gain ground. Perhaps my opponent wasn't used to his fights dragging on for so long. Maybe he didn't have the stamina that I did. Eventually he began to look as tired as I felt. With that realization, I rallied and seized the tiny window of opportunity his slowing pace provided me.

I doubled my jabs, knocking his head back like a speed bag in a sparring room and then took the attack to his body. I switched it up, landing punches up and down his body, leaving him bloodied, bruised, and swollen. The thought that I might actually beat this guy put a bounce back in my step. I felt good, like I could go another eight rounds, but my confidence was short-lived. I got sloppy and left an opening.

The Blood Pack wolf saw it and jumped, lunging in with a superman punch that landed on my jaw, fracturing it in two places and dislocating it in another.

Pain burst through my head, while blood welled in my mouth and dripped down my chin. I was spent with that blow and in danger of losing the fight. Worse than that, if I couldn't beat two wolves from the Deofol pack, there was no way I could take on their Alpha or their damned god. Not in the condition I was in, injured, dehydrated, and malnourished.

Bjorn had done the bare minimum to keep me alive and like a fool in love, I had played right into his hands.

Fuck me.

CHAPTER 17
TALIA

To my substantial surprise, Valerie kept her word. After the blessing ritual and reception that followed, she took me back to the kennels to see Galen—but his crate was empty.

"Victor told me that Galen suffered a serious injury in your last escape attempt. Perhaps they took him to the infirmary?" Valerie suggested and offered to escort me.

Eager to find my mate, I followed, pushing her to quicken her pace. When we arrived the lights were off, and the doors locked and there was no one inside. I dragged Valerie to the next building, and then another, and another. All of which turned up nothing.

We continued our search, which felt more like a wild goose chase than anything else, until word finally reached us from a passing pack member in the snow, that Bjorn had organized another tournament in celebration of my return.

Another tournament?

And Galen was nowhere to be found... A pit formed in my stomach. Galen's absence from the kennels suddenly made sense.

The pack had gathered in another large metal building that Valerie said was used to train the Deofol pack's security detail. It was also where challenges for pack rank were held.

The crowd's excitement spilled out onto the snow packed ground when we opened the door to the training facility. We were met with raucous shouts and a thunder of applause. Underneath the cheers and clapping hands, I heard the distinct sounds of two men fighting for their lives.

"Talia, wait!" Valerie urged as she struggled to keep up.

I snaked through the crowd placing bets at a table near the entrance.

"Slow down!"

I ignored her and quickened my pace. And all too soon the truth was revealed and just as I feared. Galen was in the midst of a fight—not the first from the looks of it—and seemed to be in danger of losing. I ran toward the makeshift boxing ring in the center of the room.

"Stop! Please, stop. He's going to kill him!" I shouted at the top of my lungs, but my cries for mercy were drowned out by the overzealous crowd stomping their feet on the metal risers. I pushed my way through a cluster of people who must have been unable to secure a seat in the packed risers and rushed to Bjorn, who sat ringside, and collapsed at his feet. "You can stop this. Please." I begged on hands and knees for mercy for my mate.

Galen had already taken more abuse at the hands of my mother's packmates than any wolf should rightly have to endure. I couldn't sit by and watch him suffer more pain. Not when they kept him injured and in a weakened state, unable to fight and defend himself the way I knew he could.

"That's a good look for you, Princess. I do believe our god will approve." Bjorn's upper lip curled in a sadistic grin. "Don't worry, Stefan looks ready to finish the fight. He'll put an end to Galen's suffering."

My heart burst into flame and a strangled sound crept from my lips before I found the words I needed to say. "If I accept my place in the Bone Pack and claim my throne, will you spare him?" I bowed my head and pressed my hand on the top of Bjorn's tan suede boot. "Please, Alpha, as Princess of the Bone Pack, I am asking you to show mercy to Galen. Let him live."

I chose my words carefully and made a conscious effort not to refer to Galen as my mate. Bjorn needed to believe that I was willing to give him up in order to save his life. And I was. I loved Galen enough to save him from himself—and from me. If I had to walk away from him to do that, I would.

"Enough!" Bjorn stood and walked to the edge of the mat, one hand raised above his head. "The fight is over. Our princess has declared the winner."

A few of the pack members growled, muttering their discontent over the decision to stop the fight early and spare Galen from suffering any further injuries.

"Silence!" The Deofol Alpha barked at his members, pulling rank as well as the pack bonds that gave him control over his wolves. "The Blood Pack is victorious. Their champion brings honor to their pack." He turned to some of his guards before glancing sidelong at Galen. "Take him to the clinic and get him cleaned up."

The show was officially over. Spectators climbed down from the risers, and the crowd in the training facility thinned.

"What are you going to do with him?" I asked, my heart in my throat. I hadn't given my plan to stop the fight much thought beyond saving Galen from taking another beating because of me and had failed to negotiate for the terms of his release.

How could I have been so stupid?

Bjorn clearly viewed Galen as a threat, if not to his position as Alpha, at least to the pack's plan to marry me off to their god, so there was no telling what he'd do.

"I'm not going to do anything with him," Bjorn answered as he combed his fingers through his thick, white beard. "You've claimed your birthright, your place among the Bone Pack, and your crown. What happens to him now is up to you."

"Are you serious? After all this? The beatings, the starvation, and locking him up in a crate with dogs? You're just going to let *me* decide his fate?" I didn't even bother to hide my feelings of disbelief or mistrust.

What is he playing at?

Bjorn had proven himself to be a cruel leader and less than honorable. The fight he'd arranged between Galen and the two wolves instead of accepting the challenge himself proved that. He was more than willing to take on a severely wounded man and call it a fair fight. I would be a fool to take him at his word.

"You've accepted your fate," Bjorn said simply and parted the slit in the sleeve of my dress and touched the demon mark on my wrist. It was darker and more pronounced than the last time I'd checked not an hour before in the bath. "This proves it." He traced the sigil with his finger before adjusting the fabric of my sleeve and covering the mark. "There's nothing your boyfriend can do about it, no matter how much he loves you—or you love him. You saved him and you can keep him alive and in good health by reminding him of that."

"So, what happens now?" I asked, flabbergasted that it could all wrap up so neatly. "I stay here and fulfill my duties and he's free to just go about his life? No harm, no foul?"

"Something like that. What's keeping him here, apart from you?" Bjorn shrugged my question off. What happened to Galen was of no consequence to him anymore. He had gotten what he wanted. "I'm sure Valerie explained the concept of a queen's consort. The question is, do you want that life for him? Does he want that?"

"No." I couldn't speak for Galen, truthfully, though I

suspected I knew what his answer would be. Still, even if he wanted to stay here with me at the ends of the Earth, I wouldn't let him. He had a pack to lead, people who loved and depended on him. The Long Claw pack needed their Alpha back. He had a future back home, with or without me in it.

And I won't take that away from him.

"Then you know what to do." He wiped his hands together, as if he was washing away dirt and grime, but I knew he was washing his hands of Galen. "You threw yourself at my mercy and declared your intention in front of the pack. What happens to him now is up to you. Not me, Princess. But know this, Talia... if you betray me, your pack, or our god, we won't kill you. We'll kill him and everyone he cares about."

Bjorn clasped his hands on my shoulders as if he were an old family friend, held my gaze, and gave them a gentle squeeze. "I think we understand each other now." Then he turned and walked away, leaving me standing alone at the edge of the blood-stained mats.

"Princess!" Valerie called out, pushing her way through the last of the stragglers to catch up to me. "Princess, are you all right? Talia?"

"Sorry, I'm still not used to people calling me that. I'm not sure if I'll ever get used to it." I had turned around, acknowledging her only when she called me by my name.

"You will, in time. I couldn't get through the crowd." Valerie waved her hand, gesturing to the room that was slowly emptying of pack members now that the fighting was over. "That was brave of you, approaching the Alpha the way you did."

"No, it wasn't. There was nothing brave about it." I hadn't truly risked anything. Not when Bjorn couldn't or wouldn't hurt me. Of course, he could still use Galen to hurt me... and that's exactly what he'd done.

"Damn it," I exclaimed, curling my hands into fists at my side, crescent moon indents forming in my palms from my fingernails.

"What? What's wrong?" Valerie scanned the room, searching for a new threat. But the threat was over. The battle of wills was over. Bjorn had already left.

"Nothing. I just got played, that's all," I growled, angry with myself for falling right into Bjorn's trap.

The Alpha had cleverly played the long game, moving his pieces around the chess board, until, in the end, he had taken the queen.

Check mate.

"I'm sorry, I don't understand." Valerie's brows pinched together, her eyes clouded in obvious confusion. "Who played you? How?"

"Never mind. It doesn't matter now." I wrapped myself more tightly in my fur cloak and headed for the medical building.

Bjorn had achieved what he wanted. Vindication. After my mother had run away, a blight lingered over his reign as Alpha. I got the distinct impression that she was the very first wolf to defy him. And faced with me, he'd refused to have another, of the same line, the very same blood, do as she had done. In using Galen to manipulate me, he had just made sure of that. His reign as unchallenged Alpha was finally and unquestionably secure.

I'd done what my mother had so ardently refused to do. I had just claimed my heritage, accepting my place in the Bone Pack and my title as princess and would now be forced to marry the demon wolf god whether I liked it or not. But I still had one last trick left up my sleeve. One final play that could potentially knock all the pieces off the board and make this right.

"Where are you going?" Valerie called after me. "The medical building? I'll come with you."

"I'd rather go alone," I called back, quickening my pace. Pushing open the door to the outside world of ice and snow, I covered my face with my arm to block the blast of cold air that threatened to steal my breath and crystallize the very air in my lungs.

"I think it's probably for the best if I go with you! You're a true princess now and while Bjorn is happy you've stepped into your role and accepted your responsibilities, I can think of at least a few people who might not be." Valerie stuck to me as if she'd been super glued to my side and matched my pace.

"Let me guess, the runners up in the princess pageant?" I pulled the cloak's hood over my head, tugging it down past my brow and tucked my chin against my chest. I pressed on, fighting the arctic wind as I walked. "All right, fine. You can come with me." I'd already had my ass handed to me by Bjorn and had no desire to add my being literally stabbed in the back to the ever-growing list of horrible things that'd happened since we arrived in Prudhoe.

"Safety in numbers," Valerie said with a smile and dipped her chin, leaning into the wind as she walked.

Ice crystals formed on the tips of my eyelashes, while my lips and the tip of my nose went numb before we reached the clinic. I cupped my hands in front of my face and huffed out a warm breath of air, catching it in my palms to thaw myself out. The wind was relentless and the cold intolerable. It settled into my bones, but unlike the residents of Boot Hill, it hadn't settled into my heart.

At least not yet.

The clinic's air lock door hissed as we entered the building. An oscillating space heater kicked on and blew warm air around the small waiting area. Five chairs lined two adjacent walls and met in the corner. End tables with magazines piled on top were situated at both ends. It looked like any other waiting room at any other express care center.

It looks normal.

Except Boot Hill was anything but normal. It was a place where the old ways meshed with modern times.

"Can I help you?" A round middle-aged woman dressed in bright pink scrubs with a white thermal underneath, stepped through a swinging door and dropped into a half curtsey. "Princess, I'm so sorry. I didn't realize—"

"Please, you don't need to do that, and you have nothing to apologize for." I loosened my cloak, pushing it back off my shoulders to prevent me from overheating inside the heated clinic. "A man was brought in here earlier..."

"Your friend, Galen." The nurse put a notable and heavy emphasis on the word *friend*. "Yes, he's a bit groggy from the tranquilizers. He's in and out, but he has been asking about you."

"Tranquilizer?" Perhaps I'd spoken too soon. She might have had something to apologize for after all. "Why on Earth would you tranq him?"

"He was pretty out of it when they dropped him off. I don't think he realized we were trying to treat him, not hurt him. He was trying to fight us." The nurse flicked her gaze to the reception desk and the phone that was ringing off the hook. "He's in room four, Princes. Please, if you'll excuse me."

"Would you mind, Valerie?" I asked, gesturing to the chairs in the waiting area.

"Of course not. I don't mind at all." Valerie navigated a few children's toys scattered on the floor and claimed one of the uncomfortable looking chairs against the wall. Her annoyed expression as she searched the stack of well-read magazines said otherwise. She minded. A lot. She desperately wanted to play the role of my lady-in-waiting. She wanted me to trust her—I assumed ultimately to spy on me and gain favor with Bjorn or the demon wolf god.

She had to have an agenda. I wasn't an idiot. And if that was it, it was a solid plan, but unfortunately for her it wouldn't work because I didn't trust her as far as I could throw her.

I left Valerie in the waiting room and made my way down the hall in search of room four. "Galen?" I knocked on the second door on the right, marked with a black number four stenciled in the top center. "It's me. Talia."

"Talia, is it really you?" His voice sounded a bit warped, most likely from the injuries to his jaw. Thank God for speedy shifter healing, though it would take more than a few hours for his broken jaw to be fully healed.

I opened the door to find Galen laid up on the bed, though it looked more like an examination table than a proper bed.

He draped his forearm over his eyes, blocking them from the bright overhead fluorescent lighting, and licked his lips as if they were dry.

"Thirsty?" I pulled a small cup from a metal dispenser fastened to the wall by the sink and filled it with cold water. Luckily there were straws in a container beside the dispenser. Maybe they often had victims of fights with damaged jaws here? "Drink some water, Galen. It's just the tranquilizer wearing off that's making you thirsty."

"They drugged me?" He sipped on the contents of the paper cup until it was empty, then crushed it in his hand and tossed the wadded-up wax coated paper onto the table next to his bed. "Again?"

"They said you were fighting the nurses." I brushed sweat-soaked strands of hair matted to his face, leaned in and pressed a kiss to his forehead, taking care to avoid the cuts and swelling.

"You stopped the fight," he breathed as he clasped his hand around my wrist and brought my hand to his mouth, pressing his lips briefly against my palm. "I lost the challenge and now I've lost you too."

"No, Galen. Shhh." I kissed the corner of his mouth where the swelling had already started to go down. "You haven't lost me."

"I have, Talia." He eased me back with a gentle push. "My eyes may have been swollen almost shut, but my ears were working just fine. I heard what you said to Bjorn. I heard the deal you made for my life."

"I didn't have a choice, Galen. You would have died. I couldn't sit by and watch it happen. You mean too much to me." Much to my distress, I felt an argument brewing and didn't know how to stop it.

"I'm an Alpha, Talia." He tucked his arms against his side and propped himself up on his elbows. "You can't interfere every time I'm challenged. Not that it matters anymore. You belong to the Bone Pack—the collective Deofol pack— and a demon wolf god now. It's kind of hard to compete with that."

"It was never a competition, Galen." I closed my eyes, pinched the bridge of my nose, and reminded myself it was the effects of the tranq talking and let out a deep breath. "I have an idea," I said quietly.

"An idea?" Galen raised his voice to a near shout. "What kind of—"

"Shush, before Valerie, aka my shadow, comes barging in here! She's probably out in the hall eavesdropping as it is." I crossed the room, pressed my ear to the door and pulled in a deep breath but found no trace of her scent. I returned to the side of the gurney before speaking again. "You need to shift. I need you to heal more quickly than you are at present."

Part of me considered telling Galen about my idea while he was still loopy and less likely to talk me out of my crazy plan. The rest of me knew that if I wanted my crazy plan to work, I needed Galen at his best with his full faculties—and at my side.

CHAPTER 18
GALEN

Talia was there, in the room with me and within arm's length, but I couldn't bring myself to reach out and grab her, to hold her close the way I wanted to. I hated that she saw me this way, broken and weak. I wasn't the Alpha she needed. But she refused to believe that. She loved me. I'd been beaten and broken, but none of that mattered to her and I found myself falling more deeply in love with her than ever before.

Somehow, in the midst of our nightmare ordeal, she'd come up with a plan to free the both of us from the bonds of the Deofol pack. But she wouldn't share the details of that plan until I shifted, forcing the lingering effects of the tranquilizer out of my system and healing my wounds more quickly.

She's right. I need to heal.

I called my wolf and gave myself over to him. The shift hurt like hell, tearing already sore muscles, ripping newly knitted skin, and electrifying frayed nerves.

My wolf sat up on the exam table, panting like an eager puppy, ignoring my commands to shift back. He wanted attention from Talia, the woman and wolf he'd claimed as his mate. He yipped, nudging her hands with his snout when she tried to silence him and rested his muzzle on her shoulder when she scratched behind his ears.

I pulled on the magic that controlled a shifter's ability to shift and forced my wolf back into the recesses of my mind and soul where he lived.

When I sat in front of her, back in human form, she gave a relieved sigh and rushed in to hug me. "Galen, thank God! You look *so* much better already." She wrapped her arms around me and squeezed me tight. "I'm so glad you're okay. You were barely healed before you fought those two wolves. What were you thinking?"

"That I could get us out of here." I gave Talia one last squeeze, eased out of the hug and offered a self-deprecating smile. "Things obviously did not go according to *my* plan. So, let's hear about yours."

"Right, my plan. Valerie was helping me get ready for the blessing ceremony, and she let slip..." Talia's gaze raked over my naked body and her tongue snaked across her lower lip. "Sorry," she apologized. "It's kind of hard to concentrate when you look like that."

"Like what?" I couldn't help but tease her when she blushed.

"Naked." She closed her eyes, smiled, and shook her head. No doubt clearing away the wicked thoughts she had about me. She unfastened her cloak and tossed it to me with a chuckle. "Here, cover yourself up. We don't have a lot of time. Valerie is out there waiting for me."

"Okay, I'm decent. You can open your eyes now." I laughed, tugging at the fabric of her dress. She looked amazing in the long flowing gown, her golden-red hair pulled back in a braid. I wanted nothing more than for our problems with the Deofol pack, the demons, and the demon god to be over. Talia belonged with the Long Claw pack.

She belongs with me.

"That looks good on you, but I prefer your wolf's coat to rabbit or mink." She punctuated her starlight smile with a wink. "Okay so, my plan is to find the demon wolf goddess—"

"Wait, the demon wolf *goddess*?" I asked, utterly confused and scrambling to catch up. "There's a fucking goddess in this equation too?"

Yes, and she doesn't happily subscribe to her husband's polygamy." Talia shrugged and feigned surprise. "I mean, why wouldn't a goddess want to share her all-powerful husband with other women?" She rolled her eyes before continuing. "Anyway, according to Valerie, it's the goddess behind the demon attacks, not her husband. She's targeting areas with blood ties to the demon wolf packs and hurting mortals out of spite."

"And you want to, what? Let me guess. Go find the goddess and try to reason with her?" I had to admit, it had the makings of a good plan. Talia had collected some amazing intel from Valerie. There was just one little problem. "And how are we getting out of Boot Hill to go search for her?"

"Well, I am a princess now and that does have its privileges." Talia raised the hem of her dress and dipped into a mock curtsey.

"For you, maybe. But Bjorn isn't going to let us just wander around together. You're the demon wolf god's bride-to-be. Even with your promise, he's going to be on edge."

"I have a solution for that too, but it's not ideal." She winced and offered up phase two of her plan to reach the demon wolf goddess. "In fact, it's *less* than ideal and potentially problematic. You're not going to like it."

"Talia, just tell me what it is. I can handle it." Whatever she had to say, it was obvious she thought I would veto the idea.

She chewed on her lower lip before meeting my gaze once

more. "A princess is allowed to have a consort and all that entails."

"A consort, huh? Well, that doesn't sound so bad." I wiggled my eyebrows to lighten the mood with hopes of making it easier for her to tell me the rest of her plan.

"It's not the job description we need to worry about. It's more the length of the contract." Talia sighed and rushed through the rest of the explanation. "If we convince the goddess to help us, we win. No problem. You're still Alpha of the Long Claw pack—"

"And if we don't convince her? If we can't stop the wedding, or the demons, what then?" I suspected I already knew the answer.

"Then I marry the demon wolf god and you're my consort. Forever." She turned away from me and faced the door. "I'll understand if you don't want to help me. This doesn't take two people. I *can* find her on my own."

"Forever is a long time." I slid off the exam table and closed the distance between us, wrapping my arms around her. "It would be even longer without you to spend it with."

She went limp in my arms, the tension and nerves disappearing once she heard my response. We were in this together. All the way. I loved her too much not to see it through to the end. I'd meant what I'd said—I'd rather die than lose her.

"Galen, are you sure?" Talia spun in my arms, so we stood face-to-face. "I can do this without you. The pack back home needs—"

"The pack will be fine. They're in good hands with my Betas and if the demon goddess is upset about her husband's infidelity as you say, then there's no reason for her not to side with us. If we have a common goal, then it has at least a *chance* of working."

Talia looked up at me with those violet-sapphire blue eyes and pulled me in. Like she had every day since the moment we met.

I couldn't say no to her if I tried.

"Galen, I told you about this because I wouldn't have felt right keeping it from you, not giving you the opportunity to decide for yourself. But I assumed you'd say no, and now... you're saying yes, and I... I can't in good conscience let you do it. I can't let you give up your pack to become my bedmate. If our plan fails, that's all that awaits you!"

"You're not *letting* me do anything, Talia. I am choosing the action I wish to take." I backed her against the door, pressing our bodies together, cupped her face in my hands and kissed her. "So, what do we do now?" I asked, savoring the taste of her.

"Now, we tell Bjorn." She pressed her lips to mine, with a kiss that was far too short for my liking. "I'm sure there's some kind of ritual or ceremony that has to be done. They seem to have one for just about everything."

"Do we have to tell him right now?" I glanced around the room. "We're alone for the first time in days. My shift into wolf and back again has sped up my healing and I feel strong again. It would be a shame to waste the opportunity..." I bunched up her dress and inched it up her silky, toned legs. "And I should probably get some practice in if I'm going to be your eternal consort."

Talia bit her lip in that way that drove me crazy, before she smiled, her eyes lighting up with the gleam of a thousand stars. "Practice *does* make perfect," she conceded as she hitched her leg up on my hip, ran her hand along the hard length of me and guided my cock inside of her.

We didn't need to waste time with foreplay. Both of us had been through so much since arriving here, that the very act of touching each other, of being in each other's embrace, was just about enough to bring us to the brink. At least, that's how it felt for me, and judging by the readiness of Talia's body to receive me, she felt the same. "Talia." I whispered her name as I buried myself inside her delicious warmth over and over again, thrusting to the hilt like my life depended on it. "I love you."

"I love you too," she moaned in my ear, nipping the lobe. Her breathing quickened and muscles tightened as they began to quiver. She was close, so close to climax, and so was I.

I loved making her come, it turned me on more than anything I'd ever known. There was nothing sexier than watching and feeling her orgasm, knowing I was the driving force behind it.

Biting into each other's necks to stifle our volume, we came together, our release triggering one another to impossibly intense heights. Her pussy spasmed wildly around me, milking me until I growled against her flesh, utterly spent. Finally, weak-kneed, and jelly-legged we slid to the floor.

I pulled her onto my lap and cradled her beautifully curvaceous body against me. Now that I'd gotten the chance to touch her, to be with her again, I couldn't let go. I needed to stay connected to her. I needed to be with her whenever and however I could. Talia was like a drug, and I was whole-heartedly addicted. "I guess we should talk to the Alpha," I sighed as I nuzzled into her neck, kissing behind her ear.

"Good idea. But I think we should find you some clothes first."

"I'm not the only one who needs clothes. You might want to change into something more practical too. I don't think you're going to have an easy time of convincing the demon wolf goddess that you don't want to marry her husband if you show up dressed for a wedding..."

Talia called for Valerie and then sent her on an errand to gather clothes for the both of us, and to notify Bjorn that we needed to speak with him.

When the Deofol pack Alpha arrived, he was less than thrilled to learn I'd accepted the position as consort. "We spoke about this, Talia." Bjorn pulled her aside, gripping her arm harder than necessary.

The action made me grit my teeth behind my lips and it was a struggle to swallow my growl. But Talia had warned me against reacting to Bjorn, and she was right. We needed to keep things running as smoothly as possible, so we could get to the demon wolf goddess and hopefully enact Talia's plan.

"You said you wouldn't trap Galen," Bjorn stated. "The role of consort is no way for an Alpha to live."

"I love him, Bjorn. You and the pack need me to be the Bone Pack Princess and to be happy about it." Talia stepped back from him, jerked her arm out of his grasp and pointed at me. "This is how I do that, by having Galen as my consort. I need him here."

"I understand," Bjorn sighed as he stroked his white beard, pacing the floor of the exam room. I could almost see his conniving mind work as he tried to figure out his next move. He glanced at me and narrowed his gaze. "I'm sure he feels the same way, but with the news of his father's passing and the circumstances surrounding his death, I don't see how Galen could stay and fulfill the role of consort."

"Don't talk about Max!" Talia rounded on him, her face flushing with a mix of anger and pain. She had cared for my father and was as protective of him and his memory as I was. "An Alpha like you isn't worthy of speaking his name."

"Easy, Princess." Bjorn wasn't offended by the slight. In fact, his knowing smile said quite the opposite, as if he'd expected her to react just that way. "I knew of Max. He was a formidable wolf in his day. Which is why the manner of his death troubles me."

"He was sick," Talia retorted crossing her arms over her chest. "His body couldn't fight the infection anymore."

"Wolves don't just get sick, Talia. Especially not a wolf as strong as Max was." Bjorn scratched his cheek and jaw. "It's been bothering you too, Galen. I can see it in your eyes. The question haunts you. How did he get sick? Why couldn't he simply heal? The illness wasn't from natural causes, I can tell you that."

"And how would you be able to tell me that?" Despite my resolve not to react, my fingernails elongated, and my hands partially shifted. My temper and my wolf were getting the better of me. "If you had anything to do with my father's death—"

"The Long Claw pack wasn't a concern of ours until you brought Talia to the summit and confirmed Valerie's research. She'd been tracking down our lost princess. You simply sped up the process by bringing her out into the open like that, but we would have found her eventually." Bjorn folded his arms over his chest and widened his stance. "No, Galen, you need to look closer to home for the source of the mysterious illness that caused your father's death."

Northwood.

The thought jumped into my head, but I didn't voice it. Not now, in front of Bjorn, even though it was obvious that's who he meant. The sharp pointy ends of my canines pricked the soft tissue inside my mouth. My wolf was too close to the surface, fighting my will and pushing to break free. "How do you know this?"

"I'm isolated from the rest of the world, Galen, but not entirely cut off. Word reached me from the summit. There was speculation around your father's death after you and Talia left the meeting." Bjorn's lips parted in a satisfied smirk.

I didn't smell a lie. He spoke the truth or believed he did, but he wasn't offering it out of the goodness of his heart. He didn't want me with Talia, even as her subject or consort. Bjorn wanted me out of the picture entirely and information about my father's death and the Northwood pack's possible hand it in was a good way to do it. But I saw the play for what it was.

"My father was at peace in the end. He died in his sleep, and I buried him. That was the end of Max. Nothing I do will change that now." It pained me to say those words, but I put as much conviction into them as I could to convince Bjorn I would not leave Talia. I would have my vengeance on the Northwood pack, but not until Talia was free and safely away from the demons of her past.

It was a gamble. If things went wrong, I would lose everything. My freedom, my pack, and the future Talia and I were meant to have. But she was worth the risk and I was more than willing to roll the dice for our love.

CHAPTER 19

TALIA

T he news that Max's death had been a homicide rocked Galen to his core and sent him reeling back to the moment he received the call about his father's death.

I recognized the haunted look in his eyes and the pain etched in the lines of his face. I'd helped nurse his spirit back to health and helped him through the grieving process once. I knew I could do it again and I would. I'd do anything for Galen. But we didn't have the time or luxury to work through it the way we had the first time. Galen needed to come to grips with the information and his new reality sooner rather than later, because I needed him at my side for our plan to work.

Galen had agreed to be my consort. He put his trust in me and in my plan to find the demon goddess, and in doing so had put his life on the line. The proverbial clock was ticking.

"You heard him," I said, straightening my spine to stood toe to toe with the Deofol Alpha. "He's made his choice."

"I heard him, but I just don't believe him." Bjorn shook his head and spat on the floor by Galen's feet. "If someone murdered my father, I wouldn't rest until I'd spilled every last drop of blood from their body."

Galen's muscles tensed, his body jerking as he struggled to keep his wolf in check.

"My consort and I will return to my room," I announced as I took Galen by the hands and led him out of the exam room. "Valerie, we're leaving. Take us back to my room." I wasn't sure how to get to the building my room was in from the clinic. I should have paid better attention to my surroundings when Valerie escorted me to the training facility; then I wouldn't have had to rely on her so much.

Of course, my surroundings were covered in snow and, apart from the meeting house, the buildings all looked the same. Galen and I were stuck with Valerie at least for the time being. We bundled up in layers of the cold weather gear that Valerie had brought for us and followed her out into the elements and to the main living quarters.

A storm was on its way and moving in fast. Flurries had already started to fall, and blizzard conditions were expected within the hour Valerie informed us. Our plans to track down the demon wolf goddess would have to wait until the snowstorm moved out to sea the following day. Weather changed on a dime here, and there was no use fighting Mother Nature.

Still, the extra day to mull over our plan and talk wasn't necessarily a bad thing. It would give Galen more time to come to terms with what Bjorn had hinted at about his father's death. And there were plenty of ways to spend the hours stuck in my room—all of them involving Galen in my arms. The lack of our bond these past few days had been nothing short of torture. Having had him in my heart and mind had become second nature, and having it severed and stolen away almost physically hurt.

Valerie dropped us off outside my bedroom and went to the commissary to prepare a proper meal for us. I'd instructed her to double his portion. He needed the extra protein and carbs after the injuries he'd sustained and the way he'd been held in the kennel cage for so long. He was already dehydrated and malnourished. Healing those wounds had already cost an exorbitant amount of calories he couldn't afford to lose.

Galen lit a fire in the small wood burning stove in the corner of my room and curled up on a pile of pillows on the floor in front of it. He stared at the flames, flickering behind the small glass window, seemingly lost in his thoughts.

I left him to them, giving him a few minutes alone. He'd share them with me when he was ready.

A soft knock sounded at the door not long after. Valerie stood outside in the hallway balancing three trays with food piled on top of each.

I relieved her of her burden and excused her for the rest of the night. "Are you hungry?" I asked as I juggled the serving trays. Crossing the room, I set them on the floor beside Galen.

Dried fruits, meats, roasted nuts, slices of cheese, and fresh bread spilled over the sides of the plastic trays. I longed for a hot meal, like a hearty stew or a rare, seared steak and a big old baked potato, but beggars couldn't be choosers. Especially not in the Arctic Circle. Besides, there was plenty of protein and nutrient rich foods to help Galen regain his strength; and that was what mattered most. I handed him a piece of jerky, waiting for him to take a bite, and went back for the bottles of water on the dresser that Valerie had stocked when I'd first been given the room. "Here." I twisted the cap off the bottle and handed it to him. "You need to rehydrate."

"Thanks." Galen took the bottle, tipped his head back and guzzled down all sixteen ounces in one impressive gulp. "I made the right decision. I know I did," he said.

"You loved your father, Galen. He was a great man and your best friend. It's completely normal to have doubts after learning what we did. I'd be shocked if you didn't." I covered a crusty piece of bread with a slice of soft cheese and handed it to him, forcing him to eat. "But it's not too late to change your mind, Galen. I'm sure Bjorn would be only too happy to release you of your obligation and arrange for a plane to take you right back to the pack."

"Oh, I'm sure he would. He'd definitely be happy to get rid of me," Galen replied around a mouthful of food. "It's what he wants. He wouldn't have bothered to tell me about my father unless he had something to gain. A wolf like Bjorn doesn't do anything without an ulterior motive. It's how he's remained in power so long. He not just strong, he's a thinker—a manipulator."

"While all that's true, it isn't a reason to stay." I clutched my water bottle, the thin plastic crinkling under my grip, and did my best to hide the fear that he would choose to leave me. But the last thing in the world I wanted was for Galen to stay out of some warped sense of duty.

"No, but *you* are. I meant what I said to Bjorn." He brushed the breadcrumbs from his hands and reached for me. "Going home isn't going to bring my father back, and you know what they say... revenge is a dish best served cold. I'll make sure the Northwood pack pays for what they did, if what Bjorn says is true. But that can wait. The demon wolf goddess can't. Not if we stand any chance of making this work."

"If you're sure this is what you want," I said, creating yet another opportunity for him to change his mind. Each time I did it, it hurt and brought on a new wave of fear and anxiety, but I knew what it felt like to be trapped—and I'd never do it to him.

Not ever.

"What I want is you, Talia." Galen pushed the trays of food out of the way and tugged me to him. "It's the only thing I'm sure of right now."

"It's just, I know how much is riding on this plan and how slim our—"

170

"Don't," he urged, pressing his finger to my lips. "Don't doubt yourself or us. We're going to find the demon wolf goddess and she's going to help us. Everything is going to work out."

I hoped with all my heart he was right, that *I* was right, because our lives depended on it.

Galen's hands skimmed down my side, slid under the layers of my clothes and brushed against bare skin.

His touch electrified me. The brief encounter we'd shared at the clinic barely took the edge off the ache of desire pooled inside me.

He stripped away the layers of clothes that separated us, his touch rougher and more hurried once my body was exposed to his view. He kissed his way down my neck, leaving a trail of fire in his wake. Reaching my breasts, he cupped them with both hands, before squeezing and rolling my sensitive nipples between his thumbs and forefingers. Without hesitation Galen adjusted his position, moving on top of me, and nudged my legs apart with his knee.

I opened myself to him, gasping when he pressed the hard length of his cock against my pussy. "Galen, please. I need to feel you inside me," I begged, needing that connection with him more than I needed air in my lungs. "I missed you so much... when I couldn't feel you..."

"I know. It was the same for me." He ground his hips, sliding his shaft up and down my warm flesh, teasing me, and driving my need to a fever pitch.

I worked my hand between us, wrapped my fingers around the base of his cock and guided him to my entrance.

In one swift movement Galen buried himself inside me, his cock forging a path through me like a sword through flesh.

My back arched and my hips thrust up to meet his, but it wasn't enough. Not nearly enough. I wanted more, deeper, harder, faster. I wanted to feel consumed by him.

Galen gripped my hips, pinning me against the floor, and held me still. He slowed his pace, easing out to the tip, and sliding all the way back inside until he was fully buried inside me again.

The pace was maddening and slowly driving me insane. I raked my nails down his back, and grabbed his ass, pulling him toward me, pleading for him to give me what I wanted.

Galen held back, waiting until I conceded and gave control over to him. "Is this what you want, baby?" He thrust hard.

I cried out loud in response, begging him for more.

He picked up his pace, pumping faster and harder, and gave me exactly what I needed.

"Oh, God, Galen. Yes, yes! Don't stop." I wrapped my legs around his waist and hooked my feet at the ankles, my hands splayed across his chest as I gazed up into his eyes. My muscles tightened around him, on the edge of an agonizing climax. I felt him throbbing inside me.

His heart raced and his breathing was ragged. He was close too, ready to come and join me in ecstasy.

That was enough to push me over the precipice and into the most intense orgasm I'd experienced in my life. I clawed at him as I rode the waves of pleasure that crashed within me, my own breathing labored as I squeezed my eyes shut tight, focusing on the sensations assaulting my body.

Galen finished a moment later with one final thrust, his strong thigh muscles quivering between my legs as the last tendrils of his pleasure surged through his body. "Holy shit, that was intense." He collapsed beside me, panting and slick with sweat, his molded to mine.

"I love the way you make me feel, Galen. Sex with you is—" I sighed, searching for the words only to fall short. "I don't even know. I can't even put it into words." I wasn't sure the right words existed to describe just what I felt for Galen or the things he did to me.

"You're my mate, Talia. I intend to spend the rest of my life making you feel this way." Galen wrapped his arms around me, pulling me even more tightly against him as he nuzzled into my neck.

His warm breath tickled the sensitive skin behind my ear. I lay there, wrapped in the cocoon of his arms and legs, relishing the love I felt with his body pressed to mine, until his limbs went slack, and sleep claimed him.

He needed the rest. I'd exhausted him, expending yet more of his much-needed calories when I was supposed to be replenishing his body, not draining it further. I had a sneaking suspicion that he would say it was well worth it.

I eased out of his arms, careful not to wake him, and tiptoed to the bathroom, inching the door closed shut behind me. After answering nature's call, I took a quick shower and then drew a luxuriously hot bubble bath with the hope that Galen would soon awaken after a power nap to join me in a nice, long soak. But my hopes of a romantic bubble bath were dashed by the muffled sound of snoring through the bathroom door. The sound made me grin as a surge of love for my mate rose up within me. I figured we could always have another bath together when he finally woke up.

I twisted my hair into a messy bun on the top of my head and stepped over the edge of the tub. My toes pierced the layer of bubbles, reaching the near scalding water below, when I caught a glimpse of something moving in my peripheral vision. "Galen?" I said instinctively, my brow furrowed. I withdrew my foot and turned, expecting to see the door open and my mate leaning against the jamb watching me with lust-filled eyes, but no one was there...

The door was still firmly closed. Everything in the bathroom was the same. Nothing was out of place, and I was alone. Or so it seemed. But I couldn't shake the feeling that someone was watching me. My heart rate increasing, I wrapped myself in a towel and flicked the switch to turn on the light bar above the sink, doubling the available light in the bathroom and reducing the shadows to near-zero. I scanned the small room for something or someone.

That's when I noticed it. The lock on the doorknob had been turned sideways to the engaged position. "Show yourself," I growled out, gripping the ends of my towel, and holding it in place while I spun around and yanked open the linen closet door, attempting to surprise whoever was hiding inside. But there was no one there.

"Hello, Princess." Hot, acrid breath skated across my shoulder and wafted up to my nose, tripping my gag reflex.

I retched instinctively, unable to help myself at the intrusive stench of brimstone and sulfur.

Laughter skated over my skin. "Now, is that any way to treat a friend?"

I turned on my heel toward the sound of the voice, but again, no one was there.

"The master's been waiting for you." Fingers brushed my skin, tracing a line from shoulder to wrist.

I jerked back, tripped on the bathmat, and stumbled into the bathroom counter, knocking over the beauty products that Valerie had stocked for me. Bottles crashed against the marble countertop and rolled to the floor and glass shattered on impact with the tiles.

"Talia?" Galen called out, his voice still groggy from sleep. "Are you okay in there?"

"Tell him you're fine." What felt like the tip of a knife pressed through the towel against my spine. "Tell him to go back to sleep, or I'll sever your spinal cord and then move on to your boyfriend. You'll heal, don't worry. I can't have you paralyzed when I take you to the master, but your little prince out there? I'll ensure he's dead."

Finally, I recognized the voice hissing in my ear. Shock burst through me, roiling the heat of betrayal through my veins. "Darius?" I whispered? Too many questions swirled in my brain and I couldn't focus on just one.

Where did he come from? How did he find the Deofol pack, and managed to slip inside the encampment unnoticed? How had he gotten inside my bedroom? And was he there the whole time, watching Galen and I make love, waiting to spring his trap?

"Tell him." Darius rasped against my ear, jabbing the point of the blade into my back, the tip piercing my skin.

"I'm... it's all right... Just a little clumsy, I guess." I stammered my way through an explanation for the crash of cosmetics that had roused Galen from his sleep and tried not to do the same with his suspicion. "I was just about to take a bath."

"A bath, huh?" Galen's voice was closer now, just outside the door. "Nothing but a layer of bubbles between me and your naked body?"

Galen turned the doorknob, jiggling it when he discovered it was locked. "The door's locked, Talia."

"He's defiled you for the last time. The master has claimed you. You belong to him now," Darius's whispered in my ear. He wrapped his arm around my waist and moved the hand with the knife to my neck, the blade pressed against my tender flesh, just below my jaw.

"Talia, let me in. The door's locked." He jiggled it harder and pounded his fist against the door. "Who's in there with you? I heard someone."

Galen pulled in a deep breath of air and smashed his fist against the door. "I know that voice; that scent." Galen ripped the doorknob out of the door, knocking it off its hinges, appearing in the doorway, wild-eyed. "Darius. You fucking bastard," he accused.

"My master has waited long enough." Darius increased pressure on the knife, driving the blade deeper into my neck, and sending a trickle of blood whispering down to my clavicle. "Don't move," he warned.

Galen's eyes followed the trickle of blood and his mouth tightened.

I could almost feel the effort it took him not to shift.

"I never trusted you," he snarled. "There was just something about you, too eager, too opportunistic." My mate stilled, his body unmoving, but I could sense the wheels turning inside his mind. He was studying Darius, searching for a weakness before making his move.

"I know. Your father's death was supposed to distract you, throw you off your game, but it just pulled you and Talia closer together." Darius partially shifted his hand and dug his nails into my side. They were as sharp as the knife in his other hand. "Don't even think about moving. I'll gut her where she stands."

"And risk hurting her? What will your master say then?" Galen raised his hands in a placating gesture and tried to buy us some time.

"He'll heal her," Darius sneered, piercing my side with his claws to prove his point.

I gritted my teeth, holding in the moan of pain that threatened to escape me.

"What do you want, Darius? Is there something I have that you want, something worth trading for Talia?" Galen tried bargaining with him, but it was useless.

We both knew he already had what he came for. Me.

"No," he answered simply. "I just like watching you squirm." Darius stepped back, pulling me with him. "My master is *so* looking forward to meeting his new bride," he taunted the love of my life.

I turned my head as a shadow portal opened up behind us.

Darius leaned back into the void, taking me along with him. Galen's scream of rage and despair followed me into the darkness and echoed in my ears, wounding my very soul.

Darius, the traitor, had ruined my plan to approach the demon wolf goddess in a move I couldn't have ever seen coming. Any hope of escape I had now was gone, lost in the darkness that surrounded us like a plague of hate and dark mirth against my skin.

I was about to meet the demon wolf god—my future husband. *Fuck.*

The final book in the Shifter Rejected series is available now: https://books2read.com/wolfofstarlight

Made in the USA
Las Vegas, NV
04 February 2025

17517035R00111